SAM CRESCENT

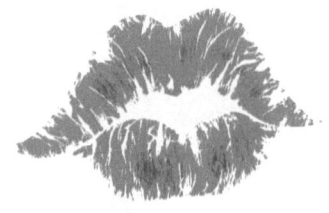

EVERNIGHT PUBLISHING ®

www.evernightpublishing.com

Copyright© 2020

Sam Crescent

Editor: Karyn White

Cover Artist: Sour Cherry Designs

Jacket Design: Jay Aheer

ISBN: 978-1-77339-375-9

SAM CRESCENT

DEDICATION

I want to thank Evernight, Stacey Adderley, and Karyn White, for their wonderful support with this series. Chaos Bleeds means so much to me and I love working on each book.

Also, I want to thank my wonderful readers for their amazing words and love toward these books.

SAM CRESCENT

CURSE'S CLAIM

Chaos Bleeds, 3

Sam Crescent

Copyright © 2014

Chapter One

Curse took a long drag on his cigarette as he watched the spritely blonde bounce on his cock. She wasn't a bad fuck, but he really wasn't into it. He couldn't remember her name, and he really didn't care. The woman groaned, pushing up and down on his cock. Her ribs were showing, and he'd watched her snort some coke before coming up to the room with him. The guys were all coming down from the rush after going to visit The Skulls in Fort Wills. Ripper had stayed behind with Judi, and Devil took his woman and two kids. It wasn't the same travelling on his bike while his President rode in a fucking station wagon. Curse didn't like it, and it wasn't right with him.

"Oh, I love your cock. It's so big and hits the right spot."

Rolling his eyes, he blew out a ring. His cock wasn't getting bigger. Losing interest in the woman, he slapped her on the ass. "Get off."

"What? Why? I want to fuck you, Curse. Do you want me to suck you off?"

"Get out. I'm not in the mood." He sat up, peeling the condom off and throwing it across the room to land in the trash can.

"Wait, what? I want to fuck you. Ashley is busy with Pussy, and you've never fucked me."

"You're giving me a fucking headache. Ashley can do whatever the hell she wants. She's part of the club; you're not. Get the fuck out before this becomes the last night you stay in the club." He glared at her until she finally left him alone shutting the door to his room behind her. Sitting on his bed, he stared at the floor thinking about a certain dark-haired waitress who refused to have anything to do with him.

For the past couple of weeks he'd been trying to get her to go out for a ride on his bike, but she wasn't having any of it. No matter what he suggested, dinner, a movie, a picnic, she turned him down. Admittedly, she turned him down gently, but she still turned him down. Ashley had warned him she was a hard nut to crack. Mia Brown wouldn't simply give up or give in. She didn't have any other lovers waiting around for her. What he found out about Mia came from Ashley, but neither woman was very forthcoming.

Docking out his cigarette he ran fingers through his hair before he pulled his jeans back on. It was the middle of summer, and he left the clubhouse without a shirt. The whole place had erupted in the partying mood. He passed many of the sweet-butts in different states of undress. Pussy had Ashley completely naked and was bouncing her on his cock for plenty of the other members to see.

Death was getting his cock sucked by another. His brothers were either watching or participating, and the women were lapping up the attention. Leaving the clubhouse, Curse straddled his bike, turned over the engine and started out of the compound. There was somewhere else he wanted to be, and Mia would just be about to close up the diner.

Parking his bike, he folded his arms and waited for her to appear. The closed sign was placed on the door, and all the lights were turned off. No one was near the diner, and the town of Piston County was deathly quiet.

Ten minutes later he spotted Mia leaving the diner with a grey haired older woman talking about the customers they'd gotten that day. He stared at Mia hoping to see some sign of happiness on her face. She turned toward the road, and she was still frowning. From the way her lips were moving she was making calculations. Over the past couple of months he'd noticed she was always doing some kind of sum inside her head.

He'd asked Ashley about it. Mia was always calculating the cost of her mother's medical care to make sure she could afford the expense. Every cent she earned went toward the best care possible for her sick mother.

"I'll see you tomorrow, dear, take care." The older woman left her alone.

Mia placed her bag over her head and started to head in the opposite direction. She hadn't even noticed him.

"Hey," he said, calling out to her.

She turned, her gaze searching the darkness. "Who's there?"

Climbing off his bike, he stepped closer to her. "It's me."

"Where's Ashley? She said there was a party tonight."

"There is a party. She's with Pussy, and I'm

here." He reached out to tuck some hair behind her ear. She tensed up but didn't pull away.

"Ashley is probably having loads of fun." Mia's blue eyes were wide as she looked at him. What was it about this woman that he couldn't get her out of his mind? She was a beauty, that was for sure, but he'd never had a woman who consumed his thoughts like this. Ashley wasn't his woman, and she fucked every man at the clubhouse. He wasn't jealous of her, but the thought of anyone screwing this woman in front of him made him want to murder any man who touched her.

"I bet she is." He stepped closer, invading her space. She gasped out, staring up at him with wide eyes. Cupping her cheek, he stroked her lip feeling the softness of her skin against his palm. Her curves drove him crazy. Every time he saw her all he wanted to do was grab her, hold onto her, and never let go. He also wanted to fuck her and see if her pussy was as tight as he imagined it would be.

"What are you doing?"

"What I want." Mia wasn't pushing him away or demanding that he leave her alone. She stood perfectly still, eyes on his face as he pressed his thumb inside her mouth. Closing her lips, she shook her head. "You're going to make me work for this pussy, aren't you, baby?"

"I'm not going to make you work for anything." She made to take a step back. He caught her ass, holding her in place. She filled his hand perfectly. Squeezing the ripe flesh, he groaned.

"Fuck, you feel so fucking good."

"Let go of me. Do you have to be so crass?" Mia wasn't pushing him away, but she wasn't embracing him either.

His cock tightened at the feel of her body next to his.

"No. I'm not letting you go. As for the other, this is who I am, baby. Get used to it." Curse stroked the curve of her ass then moved on to the other cheek. He loved the feel of her filling his hands.

"What do you want?" she asked.

Staring into her eyes Curse thought about what he wanted. The only answer he could come up with was her. He wanted Mia, and he didn't care what he had to do to get her.

"I want you."

"I'm not for sale. You can't just request me with the hope of getting me in your bed." She frowned as she answered.

"All women have a price. How much money do you need?" he asked. He'd be willing to pay whatever it was to get her.

"Money? You seriously think I'll sleep with you for money?"

"Sleeping is not on my mind. Sex, hard, rough, and hot is what I've got in mind. I'm willing to pay anything to get you." Sinking his fingers into her hair, he inhaled her floral smell. He didn't know what she smelled of, only that it drew him in and was utterly addictive.

"I don't have time for this. I need to get home to take care of my mother." She finally put her hands on his chest and pushed. He took a step back, reluctantly releasing her body. Curse knew all about her mother and the cancer she was fighting. Breast cancer was an awful thing, and Mia's mother had lost both of her breasts and undergone an intense treatment of chemotherapy. The cancer was gone, but at the moment she was always sick and the doctors were prescribing a lot of medication, all of which cost money. Mia was spending money on her mother, and she didn't even know if it would keep her alive for longer.

The money they would have had if her father hadn't run away with his younger secretary. Still, her mother was a darling. He visited her once with Ashley when Mia was busy working at the diner. From what he learned she was always working and never having any fun. She came to one of the parties the club held but never stayed too long to mingle.

Her mother wanted her to go out and have fun, but Mia wouldn't have any of it. She took a step away from him, stopped and turned to glare at him. "I'm not a whore. I don't go screwing men for money."

"I wouldn't call you a whore, just desperate for money."

"I can take care of myself. Stop bugging me. Nothing is going to come of it."

Stepping closer, he sank his fingers into her hair pushing out the clips that she'd bound her hair with. He cupped her hip with his other hand. Claiming her lips, he moaned as she cried out. Slamming his tongue deep into her mouth, he deepened the kiss, holding her tight.

His cock threatened to split his jeans, he was that hard. She started to push him away, fighting him. Curse refused to let her go. In a matter of moments she stopped fighting him. Her hands gripped his shoulders before moving up to wind around his neck.

Not moving, he drew her closer to him. His cock pressed to her stomach, making his need known to her.

****

Mia needed to stop. This man before her was deadly. He'd take over everything she ever knew and consume her body. Every time he came around, he made sure for her to know his intentions. Now he was offering money for her to sleep with him. What hurt the most was the temptation of earning more money. She hated it.

Working at the diner and cleaning houses whenever she got the chance, she still struggled to make ends meet. Her mother's prescriptions, medical bills, and living expenses were making it impossible for her to keep up with expenses. If she was ever poorly and needed time off work then she'd be screwed. Her life was all about living on the edge of surviving. Ashley tried to help her out, but Mia couldn't accept any money without working for it.

Curse's tongue met hers, and she was lost. He wasn't wearing a shirt, and his entire ink covered chest was on display. His arms were so thick that as he held her, she felt delicate in comparison.

His cock pressed against her stomach. The waitress uniform she wore didn't hold much protection against his searching cock.

"Are you wet for me, baby?"

Sinful words that she knew she couldn't fall for. Biting her lip, she shook her head. "No."

"You're lying to me. I don't like being lied to."

He walked her back until she was pressed against the brick wall. Most of the town was nervous around the Chaos Bleeds crew whereas they didn't bother her. They were part of the town like the drugs and prostitutes were. Since her father abandoned them, she'd learned not to care what other people felt. The Chaos Bleeds crew was not dangerous unless women wanted to stay virgins. She was used to men giving her the once over then moving onto Ashley. Her friend loved men and the attention she got whereas Mia always liked her own space.

Having a boyfriend had never appealed to her as they wanted time, time she couldn't afford.

"I'm not lying to you."

"Yes, you are. Let's see, shall we?"

She never expected him to find out. The waitress uniform came down to her knees. The hand on her hip slid under her uniform. He skimmed her inner thigh with his fingers.

"What the hell are you doing?"

"I'm going to see if you're lying to me. I hate being lied to." His palm cupped her pussy, and he cursed. "And you've been lying to me."

Tell him to stop. Shout at him, curse, and get him away.

He moved her panties aside and ran a finger through her slit. The instant he stroked across her clit, she was lost.

Gripping his arm, she closed her eyes at the sudden onslaught of sensation.

"You're dripping wet for me, Mia. What should I do to you?" he asked.

"Please." It had been so long since she'd been touched intimately. The last man she'd had sex with was a guy at college. He'd been shocked by her lack of commitment. She didn't want a lifetime commitment, only sex.

"Do you need to come?"

"Yes." There was no point in arguing. Curse had made sure to get what he wanted.

Opening her eyes, she looked over his shoulder. No one was there to see what was happening. She didn't care what people thought. What she hated was for others to see her need. She was used to being the woman who didn't need a man or want a man. There was only so much she could get with her own hand.

Two fingers slid across her clit then down to fuck inside her pussy.

"You're not a virgin, are you?"

"No."

"Ashley seems to be under the assumption that you are."

"I didn't fuck anyone in high school. I waited until college."

"Any man in sight?"

"No, none."

She cried out as he pinched her clit. "We shouldn't be doing this," she said.

"I don't care what we shouldn't be doing or should. You're going to come against my fingers and stop complaining."

Mia opened her mouth ready to argue, but he took her mouth stopping her from talking.

Breaking the kiss, she moaned as his lips moved down her neck. "This doesn't mean I'm going to sleep with you."

"I don't want to sleep with you. I want to fuck you, nothing else."

It was like he'd walked straight out of her fantasies. No commitment, only fucking.

Wrapping her arms around his neck, she thrust onto his fingers. The lust took over, and she pressed her lips to his. Anyone could walk past them and they'd only see them making out against the brick building.

No, she didn't just want to make out.

Releasing one arm, she caressed down his body to cup his cock. She fought with his jeans, releasing the button then sliding the pants open and pulling out his cock. Curse hissed against her ear.

"What are you doing?" he asked.

"What do you think? You want to fuck as much as I do." Taking a step to the left, she moved around to the back of the building. There was nowhere else for her to go, but they were plunged into darkness. "I'm offering it to you now."

She didn't know what had come over her. Curse made her feel dangerous no matter how much she tried to fight it. With him half naked and his lips on hers, she couldn't fight the need constantly building up inside her. He came to her offering temptation. She noticed the touches he always made sure to give her. His fingers stroking her inner wrist as he took something from her hands or the way he touched her thigh before she walked away from the table. Ashley told her about his interest, but she'd not believed it.

Staring at him, she waited for his decision. She would never be the kind of woman to settle down. Watching her parents fight at every turn hadn't given her a good start in life, and then for her father to walk out with a younger model had cemented in her mind that she was never going to marry or settle down.

Curse stepped closer. The fire in his gaze had her gasping for breath. "I'll take you anyway I can fucking get you."

His hands went underneath her uniform, and he lifted her up. She gripped his arms shocked by the ease with which he lifted her. Mia was under no illusions that she was a slender woman. Her bones were covered with a nice layer of thick flesh. Her weight had never concerned her. She didn't have the time to be concerned about her weight.

Thinking over her life, Mia could dissect her life easily. Childhood to high school was obviously filled with the love that a young girl has for everything around her. Then in high school she was too busy getting her grades, sitting down for long hours, studying. She didn't have time or even cared to think about her weight. After the incident prom night with Ashley, she'd spent as much time with her friend until she went away to college.

Four years in college, she studied and worked her ass off to support herself. Her father, at the time, would only support so much, and already he was withdrawing from her. On her final year, her mother got sick, her father left, and for the last three years she'd been supporting her mother through everything. She hadn't finished college yet. Her life was on hold in order to care for her mother and get the medical bills paid before she could start living life again.

In one tug Curse tore the panties from her body. She stroked his flesh as he settled between her thighs. Staring into his brown gaze, Mia was lost. Refusing him was the last thing on her mind.

"You want me to fuck you against the wall." He pushed her hand out of the way. Placing her palm on his shoulder, she felt the tip of his cock sliding through her slit. The tip aligned with her entrance.

"Yes," she said. "There's nowhere else for us to go."

He slammed to the hilt inside her, taking her by surprise. She cried out as he growled. His mouth went to her neck, and he sucked on her flesh. Closing her eyes, she whimpered at the length of him. Curse was long, thick, and wide. The instant shot of pleasure took her by surprise.

The few times she'd had sex she was left disappointed with the feel of a man inside her.

"So fucking tight and hot." He lifted her off his cock only to slide back inside her. Keeping her gaze on his, she bit her lip to stop herself from crying out. Curse fucked her hard against the wall. Her uniform saved her from the pain, and he was as careful with her as possible. The feel of him inside her took her completely by surprise. Wrapping her arms around his neck, she held on all the way as he fucked her. The only sounds in the night air to be heard were their heavy breathing.

"Kiss me," he said.

Dropping her lips down to his, she stroked his

plump lips with her own. He held her tight as he rammed inside. The pleasure was increasing, but she knew there was no way for her to come.

Curse plunged inside her, growling as with one last thrust he spilled his release into her body. She could have smacked her head at the lack of protection. Tomorrow she would ask about the expense of the morning after pill.

"Shit, baby, I'm sorry."

He held her, and she didn't say anything. The lust was long gone only to be replaced by her anger at her own stupidity.

"Are you done?" she asked. She felt him tense in her arms, and she cringed even though she wanted this to be over.

"What's the matter?"

"Nothing. I need to know if you're done so I can go home."

He pulled out of her body and stepped back. She watched him put his cock away. His cum slid down the inside of her thigh. Wriggling her legs, she picked up the panties he'd torn.

"Give them to me."

Her gaze on his, she placed them against his chest. "You can stop coming around now. There's no need to be curious about me."

Stepping away from him, she ignored his call as she walked home. It was for the best. Mia didn't have time for complicated males.

Chapter Two

Curse slammed into the clubhouse not caring who he woke up. All of the families would be at their own home rather than staying at the club. He was so fucking angry that anyone who started a fight was going to lose. Mia had blown his fucking world, and by the end of it she looked bored. The moment he kissed her, she fought him, and then something changed. She no longer fought him but was begging for his touch and more still.

The moment she got his cock out and moved around the building to fuck he'd been totally lost. Walking behind the bar, he snatched up the brandy and went into the kitchen. Her cunt had been tight as she gripped him, and he'd not used a fucking condom. Curse didn't even know if she was on any kind of birth control. She'd wanted away from him so fast he didn't even get a chance to bring her to orgasm. He'd been wound so tight he'd not been able to wait for her to come before he found his own release.

"Fuck," he said, opening up the fridge. He knew fuck all about her. Mia never gave any part of herself even when she was talking with Ashley. The two girls were like chalk and cheese. Neither of them shared any common ground. Their friendship was a complete mystery to him.

"Hey, oh, I thought we were getting burgled," Ashley said, walking into the room wearing nothing but underwear.

"You really think some thick fuck would risk his fucking neck to come and rob us?" Curse asked. He was pissed, beyond pissed. He was furious at himself and at Mia.

"Sorry. What's wrong with you tonight?" She brushed past him to grab a juice from the fridge. Opening

SAM CRESCENT

the bottle of brandy he glared at her.

"Your fucking friend is what's pissed me off. She's a fucking cold ice queen." He swigged down several gulps of brandy, staring at her. Ashley was partly naked, but she didn't do anything for him. His cock remained flaccid.

"Mia's a lovely woman. What did you do to her?" Ashley asked.

"Stay out of my fucking business. Let's just say you're both chalk and fucking cheese." He made to storm out of the room.

"So? What does my and Mia's friendship have to do with you? We care about each other, and we're the best of friends. Leave it the fuck alone."

"Do you even know her?" Curse asked.

"I know enough about her to know men are wasting their time if they think they can stay with her. Mia will never settle down with any man."

"You're aware she's not a virgin?" He took another long drink from the bottle. What was between these two women to cement them together?

"Yes, I'm aware she's not a virgin. Men have showed her enough attention over the years for me to know the truth." Ashley held the glass in her hand with a death grip. He watched her look over his shoulder and her throat work as she swallowed. "It's none of your business why we're friends. We are, and there's nothing you can do about it."

"I fucked her."

"Good for you and for her." There was no jealousy on her face.

"We did it up against the wall of the diner." He didn't know why he was repeating what happened, only that he needed to know more about Mia. She didn't look like the kind of woman who got off on the risk factor of being caught. He'd offered her money, and she turned him down.

"So?"

"She's your friend."

"I fuck over ten to twenty guys in the Chaos Bleeds crew. She doesn't judge me, and I'm not going to judge her on how she needs to get off." Ashley shrugged. "Just don't hurt her. Mia deserves some happiness in her life."

Ashley made to brush past him. He caught her arm and held her steady. "If she deserves so much happiness why are you not helping her pay off her mother's medical bills?"

"I am helping her. She doesn't accept charity from anyone, not even me." Ashley shrugged. "I pay off extra from her account. I stole the details from a letter I found in her possession. I do help her, Curse." She shoved him away. "She's my friend, so back off."

He watched her leave, curious to know what had gone on in the two people's lives to draw them close.

Opening his cell phone, he went up to his room and dialed the only man he knew could help.

Whizz answered on the first ring. "Hello."

"Hey, man, how are you holding up?" Curse asked. Five months ago Whizz had been taken by an enemy of The Skulls. From what Curse learned and saw, the man had been tortured and raped. Devil gave the crew updates on his progress, and the man couldn't stand to be alone. He lived in the clubhouse, with Killer and Kelsey, and even with Zero and his woman, Prue, in Fort Wills. The nightmares kept Whizz awake most nights.

"I'm doing okay. I take it this is not a social call," Whizz said. The man sounded tired even to him. Curse wished he'd not called. Whatever he wanted to know he could find out for himself.

"Maybe I should leave it," Curse said.

"You've called me up. I'm awake and alert. Just tell me what the fuck you want so I can get on with doing it." Since the attack Whizz hadn't been his carefree happy self.

"I want some information on two women." He spoke the two names giving Whizz time to write them down.

"How far back do you want me to go?"

"As far back as through high school. I'm going to find out what I need, and then I'll come back to you."

"Fine. I'll do a quick search to see if anything comes up."

"Sure, no problem."

"Is that it?" Whizz asked abruptly.

"Yeah."

The call ended. Curse stared at his cell believing he'd made a mistake. Closing his bedroom door he threw his cell on the drawer top followed by his keys. He kept the bottle of brandy in his hand.

Noise from the bed drew his attention. The woman who'd been fucking his cock earlier was lying in his bed. She smiled at him, stretching her arms above her head.

"Hey, baby. I was wondering when you were going to get back. I've missed you." She rolled off the bed and stood tall. She was naked, and her pussy was bare of any hair. Mia had a thin sheath of pubic hair covering her pussy. Curse liked his women to actually look like women.

"What the fuck are you doing in my room?" he asked, taking a long gulp from his bottle.

"I thought you'd want me when you got whatever was bugging you out of your system." She ran her hands up his body, giggling. "My pussy needs a nice big cock to satisfy it."

Images of Mia entered his mind. At the beginning she'd been so into their sex, but then when he was finished, she'd cut him off. Curse hated the fact she hadn't come. If the boys ever found out they'd make his life hell. They all had a reputation to uphold, and being good in the sack was one of those rumors they liked to keep true.

"And you think your pussy is the one that's going to satisfy me?" He brushed her off, going toward his bed. Sitting down, he kicked his shoes off.

She was not deterred by his anger. Curse couldn't even remember her name. There were so many women hanging around the clubhouse and the tit club that he forgot most of their names. He remembered the ones who were important, Phoebe, Lexie, Judi, the kids' names, and he also knew the names of The Skulls' women. The ones who deserved his respect rather than the ones he only needed to fuck.

"I can give you what you need."

Her body was all hard curves and bones. Curse wasn't attracted to her in the slightest. In fact, the sight of her skeleton turned him the fuck off.

"Get the fuck out of my room, and if you come in here again I'll have the club ban you."

"But I have to give the men whatever they want."

"This man doesn't want you. Back the fuck off, or else I'll make sure all the men keep a wide berth of you."

He stood tall, ignoring her as he headed toward his bathroom.

"Seriously, you don't want to fuck me? All men want to fuck me." She folded her arms underneath her breasts looking stern.

"Really? You think you're that irresistible? Sorry,

baby, you're sadly mistaken. There are a lot better looking women out there. Now, get the fuck out before I throw you out of the clubhouse and you walk home naked."

Going into the bathroom, he heard the bedroom door slam. He still didn't know her name and couldn't give a fuck. His thoughts returned to the raven haired beauty who he'd fucked without a condom. Before she did something to anger him, he'd have to get to her early the next morning.

****

Mia placed tea and toast onto a tray along with her mother's medication for the morning. Soon she'd be back to the peak of healthy, but until then, providing for them was left to Mia. Running fingers through her hair, she carried the tray through to the sitting room. Her mother was sat on the sofa, reading a book. She smiled the moment Mia entered. Only when her mother had the energy did she move from her bedroom downstairs; otherwise she stayed in her room.

"Hey, Mom," Mia said.

"Darling, I heard you get in a little late last night. Was everything okay?"

"Yeah, a little late in closing is all. I'm about to head out for the day. I've got several houses scheduled to clean today, and I've got to head out straight away," she said, kissing her mother's cheek. "Let me know if you need anything else."

"Honey, I hate this. You need to be out finding men and falling in love."

Smiling at her mother, Mia shook her head. "I'm happy doing what I do. Rest and get better."

She grabbed her bag and apron and headed out. Wearing a pair of ratty old jeans and a black shirt meant she could clean whatever needed cleaning. Glancing down at her watch she didn't have time to head to the pharmacy, and she marked it in her mind for later today. Owning a car was an unnecessary expense and one she couldn't afford. The sun was shining, and she pulled her hair into a ponytail as she got to the first house. Jerry was a nice man with a young wife and a couple of kids. He paid well even though she was sure he was one of the pimps in the town.

Jerry opened the door while he was on the phone.

"Sure, Devil, do what you need. I'm not in the mood for this shit today." Jerry took her arm leading her inside.

Putting her bag down by the door she bent over to grab the apron. Placing the fabric over her head, she tied up the bows on either side. The apron kept most of the dirt off her.

He finished on the call and stared at her. Pushing some strands off her face, she waited for him to talk. Every time she came to his house and he opened the door he always spent several seconds looking her up and down.

"What can I do for you today?" she asked, waiting for instructions.

"Such a waste."

She frowned at his comment, but he led her down the long entrance hall.

"My office needs cleaning today and the kitchen. My wife went crazy in there. We argued, and she made a mess before storming out yesterday. Will you clean that for me?" he asked.

"Sure."

Each household contained their own cleaning supplies. She only worked for the wealthy part of Piston County. There was no way she'd be taking on jobs where a lot of crime happened. She liked living her life without fear of being shot.

Leaving his company, she grabbed the trolley she set up and headed into his office.

Jerry was already behind the desk as she walked in.

"Do you want me to do this last?" she asked.

"No. Go ahead, work. I won't interfere."

Nodding, she got down to work. Going behind his desk she opened up the windows to allow any dust to leave the room. She ignored the man behind the desk. Picking up the duster, she went around the room, cleaning away any mess she found. Jerry paid her a really good wage to clean for him, and Mia made every effort to have his place spotless. Out of the corner of her eye she saw he was watching her. Wiping her hands down her body, she spent the next thirty minutes cleaning up his room.

"I'm going to the kitchen," she said.

"Thank you, Mia."

He always looked like he wanted to say something a little extra to her. Walking into the kitchen, she winced at the mess before her. Okay, the argument he had with his wife must have been similar to World War Three. Mess was everywhere. Wiping down the food that could go back into the fridge, she got started on work. Checking her watch, she saw she had a couple of hours left to do another two houses on her list before heading toward the diner for her lunch to evening shift.

Thinking about the diner brought thoughts of Curse and the moment they'd shared last night. He'd gotten off, and she'd wanted out of there before he got a chance to do anything more. Sex was never anything amazing for her. Every time she had sex, when it was over she felt guilty for giving in. Curse didn't make it any different. For several minutes at the beginning she'd really thought it was going to be different, but it wasn't. He left her unsatisfied, and she didn't want to stay around for anything extra.

An hour later, she knocked on Jerry's door.

"Come in." She entered the room.

"I've finished. The kitchen looks spotless once again. I had to throw some food items in the trash." She handed him a note for him to know what she got rid of. "Here, this is what I had to throw away."

He took the list. "Thank you, Mia. You're always so thorough."

"Thank you. When do you need to me to come back?" She removed the apron from her body and stood waiting. He looked her up and down once again.

"Mia, have you ever considered a career change?" he asked.

"What?"

"You're a beautiful young woman. I could find some work for you."

She frowned, looking at him. "I'm happy cleaning and working at the diner. I doubt you can give me any work I'm looking for."

"You know I handle girls along with a lot of other ventures." He stood, circling the desk to lean on the edge.

"I know the rumor."

"You're a friend of one of the women fucking Chaos Bleeds. I figure I can be honest with you. You're in a desperate situation. Those bills are not going anywhere, and you need to make good money." His hands were clasped together in front of him. "I could have those bills of yours paid in full within the year. You're a fuller woman, and there are a lot of calls for men looking for women like you."

What was it with men offering her money for sex?

"Stop, right now." She folded her arms over her chest, placing one palm in front of her to stop him from talking. "Men are in the market for fat women?"

"No, fuller women. You're not fat, Mia. I can have you earning a lot of money."

She laughed, thinking about Curse. "You're the second man within twenty-four hours to offer me money for sex."

"It's good money, Mia. I can have men there and assure your safety."

"In return I have to screw men I don't know for money."

Jerry looked at the floor. "Yes. There's no shame in it."

"Apart from the fact I'll be a whore or put it nicely, a call girl or an escort." She shook her head. "This will be the last time I call to this house. Please, inform your wife that if she wants someone to clean she can find someone else."

She turned on her heel and headed out of his office. Did she have the word desperate written all over her body? Was that all she was good for? She wanted to laugh at her situation. Well, if she did suffer with illness she could always make a living offering up her body. It was stupid. Picking up her bag, Jerry came out of his office.

"Stop, take the money. You earned this."

Staring at the money, Mia wanted to tell him to shove it.

Mom's medical bills.

Taking the notes from him, she stared into his gaze. "Thank you."

"I was not trying to insult you. You're a beautiful woman, and I know I can help you out with your situation. What your father did was wrong."

Licking her lips, she pocketed the money. "What he did was wrong, and life sucks. It does suck, but my mom is everything to me. She would hate for me to sell my body for her. I'm not going to lie to her, Jerry."

"Would you do it if it wasn't for your mother?" he asked.

"No, I wouldn't. I don't like sex enough to do it." She left his home without looking back. Mia didn't see any reason to argue. Her friendship with Ashley also meant she wasn't going to go gossiping about him. She didn't gossip about friends or anyone associated with them.

She walked down five houses to get to the next man on her list. Mia looked at the luxuriant house, and a shiver passed through her. Dale Worthington scared the crap out of her. He was older than she was by about fifteen years, and he was married, but the wife was rarely home.

Mia made her way up the driveway, taking note of the single car parked before the door. She didn't know much about the man other than he liked to watch her clean. Where Jerry looked her up and down, assessing her quality, which she knew why he did now, Dale always looked ready to pounce on her.

The front door opened, and he stood smiling at her. He was tall, muscular, and scary looking.

"Hey, Mia, I was wondering how long it was going to take."

Dale didn't move out of her way, and she ended up brushing past him to get inside. Placing her bag on the floor, she bent down to grab her apron.

A moan right behind her had her crouching down so her ass wasn't in the air. Placing the apron over her body, she turned toward him.

"Where do you need me to clean?" she asked,

dreading the answer.

"Upstairs, the main bedroom needs a clean."

"Okay."

She grabbed the cleaning supplies from the trolley and walked upstairs. He followed up behind her. Great, he was going to be inside the bedroom while she cleaned. Mia hated this one job with all of her heart.

Chapter Three

Curse sat inside the diner wondering where the fuck Mia was. The lunchtime rush was about to start, and no one would serve him. The only person he wanted to be served by was Mia. Ripper sat opposite him with Judi. The couple looked so happy even though he tried to talk them all out of coming with him today. How was he supposed to talk to Mia with these two listening in?

"How is the new house?" he asked.

Judi smiled. "It's perfect. Ripper knows exactly what I wanted." She kissed her husband, and Curse winced. Judi was still the princess of the club even though she was Ripper's old lady. He hated seeing the two making out. They were in love, and he couldn't dispute that.

"Will you be starting a family soon?"

"No, we're not ready," Ripper said. "What about you? Any news with the black-haired waitress?"

The door to the diner opened. Mia ran inside, looking disheveled. She was pulling her hair back into a ponytail. He saw her hair was still wet from a shower. She didn't acknowledge any of the women. Someone patted her shoulder and pointed toward the table. When she caught sight of him, her shoulders slumped.

I'm not going anywhere, baby.

She pulled out her writing pad. "What can I get you?" she asked.

He ordered a coffee and a burger while Ripper ordered half the menu and Judi settled on a salad.

Tapping his fingers on the counter, Curse watched her walk away. Her thighs looked so tempting as she bent over the counter to send off their orders.

"I think we know what's going on between them."

Mia left the room heading toward the bathroom.

Ignoring his friends, he went to the back of the room. Opening the toilet door, he saw Mia was washing her hands in the room.

"What do you want?" she asked, turning to face him.

"I fucked you without a condom."

"I know. I'll take care of it later. I've not had time to go to the pharmacy."

"You're not protected?"

"No. I'm clean. You're the first man I've been with without a condom. I'll deal with whatever happens." She placed a hand on the edge of the sink and looked at him. "What else do you want?"

"You didn't come last night."

"So, I've learned that I don't come with a lot of men. Don't worry, Curse, you're not the first man to leave me unsatisfied." She took a step toward him, hands on hips.

"And you think this is over?"

"You got what you wanted. Move on, find another woman to fuck. I hear the club has an endless supply." There was no emotion from her as she spoke.

"What happened between you and Ashley?"

"Nothing."

She tensed up, folding her arms in front of her.

Flicking the lock in place, he stepped away from the door. He needed to find some other way of getting her alone. "You and Ashley are the same. Neither of you are jealous of the other. You never let anyone get close to you. She's the same. Both of you have secrets."

"Do you expect me to think that you're a saint? The Chaos Bleeds crew makes extra money with the tit bar they keep open?" She smiled. "Please, I'm not a fool. Everyone has secrets."

"Some people's are darker than others," he said, taking another step toward her. She didn't back away. "How dark are your secrets?"

"You're never going to find out." She placed a palm on the center of his chest. "Back off, Curse. I'm not yours to buy or to have."

"Do you really think I'll let another man have you? You're mine, Mia."

She shook her head. "One lousy fuck does not make for you to claim me." Mia ran her hand down the front of his body. She gripped his cock, rubbing the length. "You still want more?"

"Not right now."

He took hold of her hand and pressed her against the sink. When he entered the bathroom he didn't expect to get anything out of her. She kept her emotions close to her chest. No one was getting past that wall of ice she liked to keep there. He hated not knowing her secrets and having to guess at them.

Sliding his fingers underneath her uniform he found the evidence of her arousal. "I think you protest a little too much about how much you don't want me." He leaned in close as if to kiss her but held back.

"I can be turned on by you, Curse. I just know you're not much when it comes to the follow through." She tried to pull out of his arms. He wasn't having any of it. Keeping her in place with his body, he stared down into her eyes.

"Fight me all you want. You're not going anywhere until I get what I want."

"You got what you wanted last night. I don't need a reminder."

Laughing, he slid his fingers inside her panties. Her slit was soaking wet. Pinching her clit, he saw her fight the arousal.

"You're going to fight the pleasure?"

"What do you want?"

With his free hand, he tugged on her ponytail so she had no choice but to bow her head back, exposing her neck. Curse moved from her clit, down to slide inside her tight cunt. She gripped his fingers like she'd never taken a cock.

"How long has it been since you last fucked someone?"

"Besides you last night?"

"Yes."

"A couple of years. I've not had the time to date."

"We haven't dated," he said. She cut all emotion out of her life. The only love inside her was for her mother and friend. He wanted to break into the ice and become part of that circle.

"So, do you expect me to believe you're the kind of man who wants to date?" she asked.

Adding a third finger inside her body, he pressed his thumb to her clit. She wanted to have a smart mouth? He was fine with showing her who was boss. No one, not even Mia, got the better of him.

Leaning forward he licked the line of her pulse. Her pulse was racing. Mia wasn't as unaffected as she made out.

"You do realize I'm going to find out all of your secrets and then there will be no more hiding from me."

"Why don't you back off?" Her voice was breathless as she asked.

"I don't want to." As he added a fourth finger, she cried out. Mia stayed still as he sucked at her neck. Someone knocked on the door to the bathroom. He ignored it. Staring into Mia's shocking blue eyes, he touched her pretty pussy waiting for her to explode. Her body was wound tighter than he ever imagined. There was so much stress she was dealing with, and there was no time for her to have any fun.

I'm not backing away.

Mia will be mine.

He was going to warn Ashley the next time he saw her.

Sliding his thumb over her clit, her cream washed over his fingers. She gasped out, the noise going straight to his cock. He was not leaving the bathroom until she came all over his hands and he tasted her cream on his fingers.

"You're not going to the pharmacy."

"I'm not having a child."

"You'll do as you're fucking told. No pharmacy or I'll have you chained to my bed and then you can't even make money to pay for your mother's medical bills."

He wasn't bluffing. Curse would chain her to his bed, only he'd pay for her mother's care.

"Stop this."

She was not fighting him. Her body was open for him to play with.

"No. You want this. Soon, Mia, you're not going to be able to hide from me. I'm going to know everything about you."

A whimper left her hips. He sank down, holding onto her hips to keep him steady. Tugging up her uniform, he revealed her pussy to his gaze. Tearing the panties from her body, he opened her legs wide and slid his tongue over her slit.

"Oh, fuck," she said, jerking in his arms. Licking her clit, he slid down to tongue her entrance. She was shaking in his arms, getting closer to the edge of her release. Curse kept flicking her clit.

Glancing at her hands, he saw they held the edge

of the counter in a death grip.

"Curse."

He listened to her cry his name. Staying in front of her, he caressed her clit feeling her getting closer to orgasm. She would be going over the edge of release in a matter of seconds. Her legs shook, and he kept a firm grip on her to keep her steady.

Tonguing her clit, he watched her fall apart in his arms. Her orgasm crashed through her. Curse licked up her cream, relishing the taste of her pussy. Mia was going to have to learn to get used to his touch. He wasn't going anywhere, and if she liked it or not, she belonged to him.

No man was going to touch her or know what she felt like naked.

When the tremors subsided he got to his feet and wiped his mouth. "Tonight, I'm taking you somewhere. I'll get the prescription to your mother. Don't argue with me or fight with me. You'll never win."

"I'm just supposed to accept what you want?" she asked.

"Yes, fighting with me is a waste of time."

Leaving the bathroom, Curse took his place at the table. The taste of her still in his mouth, he couldn't think of anything sweeter.

****

Exhausted, Mia didn't want to see Curse, let alone go out with him. The orgasm he gave her in the bathroom had consumed her thoughts, which she hated. No man should ever be that addictive. She couldn't even remember a single order of burgers and shakes. God, she hated her job. She hated working at the diner and cleaning for a living. Mia hated her father more. If he'd stayed then they wouldn't have struggled in paying for her mother's health care and she could have finished up her final year in college. Working two jobs and taking care of her mother took every spare moment she had. There was no time for studying. She'd been studying care and nursing, the two occupations she loved to do, but neither was going to help her right away. Funding for school came after her mother's care.

Walking out of the diner at eight, she got an hour's overtime with the influx of tourists because of the heat. She spotted Curse waiting beside his bike.

"You purposefully worked an extra hour," he said.

"I need the money, Curse. I'd work twenty-four seven if it meant my mom had the best care around the clock." She folded her arms underneath her breasts, glaring at him. Ashley told her so much about him and the club life. Mia wouldn't dream of doing anything to hurt her friend. The club meant everything to Ashley as she finally had a home.

"She hates relying on you. Your mother wants you to have a life, and she's more than happy with you spending the night with me."

"I'm not spending the night with you." She didn't spend the night with any man.

"Do you have an issue with being with men? Are you a fucking lesbian?"

Mia snorted. "That makes sense, because I don't want to spend the night with you, I'm suddenly a lesbian. It makes total sense, not."

"What's your issue? What happened to the happy-go-lucky girl working as a waitress?" he asked.

"You really want to know what's wrong with me?"

"Yeah, I'm trying here."

"Then stop trying. I don't go with men because I don't need to. I'm happy being the way I am." The lies were pouring out of her mouth. When Ashley was eighteen, their friendship had been cemented by what happened to them. Mia swore she would never speak a word of what happened, and she never had. Going away to college helped her to forget. Now that she was back in town, the memories were always there, lurking, waiting for someone to hurt them. Ashley had moved on while Mia lived with what she did every day.

Curse took a step closer to her. He didn't stop until he stood right in front of her. His breath fanned her face. Closing her eyes, she tried to focus on keeping herself neutral. When he was around her, her body was no longer her own. Whatever he did, unnerved her. His presence in the diner put her on edge, and now she knew what he felt like inside her, the yearning was only growing more.

"You're fucking lying, Mia." He cupped her cheek, tilting her head back to look into her eyes. "I don't like lies."

"What are you going to do about it?"

Why was she taunting him? He forced her to take a step back then another. Curse moved her to the spot they were in the other night. With her back pressed to the wall and Curse standing in front of her, he had her trapped.

"I can think of a whole lot of shit I can do to you."

His free hand went underneath the dress of her uniform. She tensed as he palmed her ass. "I've got a place, and we're going there now." Before she could protest, he slammed his lips down on hers. Gasping, she opened her mouth, and Curse took full advantage. If she gave an inch, he'd take a mile. Curse held her in place as he ravished her mouth and kept a firm hold on her body.

Only when he was ready to release her did he

take her hand, and lead her out to his bike. He handed her a helmet and told her to climb on.

"Shouldn't I be wearing more protective gear?" she asked.

"Just put the fucking helmet on and stop testing me."

Wanting to argue, Mia glared at him.

"If you want I can put you over my knee and spank your ass now. I've not got a problem with showing off that fine ass. It's up to you. I've not got a stellar reputation around here."

Glaring at him as she knew he'd do it, she quickly put the helmet on and then straddled his bike.

"Put your arms around my waist. You've got to hold onto me."

Gritting her teeth, she wrapped her arms around his waist. Curse pulled out of the town center and made his way toward the main road. They passed the wealthy part of Piston County where she cleaned, then down the street from the strip club Chaos Bleeds owned.

She didn't know how long they were driving until he parked up at a deserted location with lots of trees, brambles, and dirt roads. The house she faced was modest and looked like an old ranch house.

Curse cut the engine and climbed off the bike.

"Get off and give me the helmet."

Hating his attitude, she did as he asked, slapping the helmet into his palm.

"Where are we?" she asked.

"This is owned by Devil and the club. It's a place for us to get away and to have some relaxing time. No one is around, and we've got this place all to ourselves."

Great, they were going to be alone with him controlling everything.

"You've brought me here why?"

He took her hand and headed straight up the front door. She watched him unlock the door, then flick the light on before going further into the house. With no other choice, Mia followed him. He placed the helmet on the floor beside the stairs.

"Come on, you're probably starved."

Curse sat her down at the kitchen table, opening the fridge. This kind of behavior from him unnerved her. She was used to fending for herself and always being the one in control. Curse took the control from her. No one told him what to do or how to do it.

Tapping her fingers on the counter, she glanced around her. The house was simple and modest, offering a small bit of luxury away from the town.

"Pasta sound good?" he asked.

"Do you know how to cook?"

"I know how to cook pasta, nothing else."

"Then how about I cook?" She tried to offer a better solution than him cooking. He didn't look like he knew his way around the kitchen.

"No, I can cook you pasta and then you can sit and enjoy."

Sitting back in her chair, she watched him working the kitchen. The heat got to him within ten minutes, and he opened a window, removing his shirt. She was treated to a lovely view of his naked, ink-covered body. The jeans rode low on his hips giving a tantalizing view of hair leading down. She'd not seen him completely naked before even though she had felt his cock inside her.

He moved out of the way of the water splashing out of the pot when he poured dried pasta shells into boiling water. In a separate bowl he mixed a couple of cheeses together with some herbs.

Crossing her legs, Mia tried to stem the arousal

building in her body.

Let him in.

She removed the clip out of her hair and fingered out the strands.

"You're checking out my body, aren't you?"

"Yes."

"You know, I don't buy the cold bitch routine. You're nice to everyone else but me."

Mia stared down at her clasped hands on the table. Unlike everyone else, Curse threatened her whole world. The attraction between them was hard to deny even if she did think it was insane. He was handsome, could have any woman he wanted, and yet, he wanted her.

Then, she thought about his offer of money along with Jerry's offer that afternoon. Were there really men out there who'd pay for her … services?

She cut the thought off immediately. There was no way her mother would ever allow her to use her body for sex.

Would she ever know?

Facing her mother would be extremely difficult afterward. She'd rather work the two jobs than have to deal with her mother's pain of knowing why she was sleeping around.

"I don't show favoritism with customers. You come to the diner, and I'm more than happy to help." She offered him a smile.

"You came to the party when the Chaos Bleeds crew returned. The day Ripper got his ass handed to him. You danced with Pussy, Death, and Devil. None of them posed a threat to you. Yet, me, you won't give me two minutes to show you how good it can be between us." He drained the pasta, reserved some cooking liquid then poured the cooked pasta into the pot.

In quick moments, the pasta with the cheese mix was finished, and he served it up.

"There, dinner is served."

He put the plate in front of her, sitting opposite.

Picking up her fork, Mia wondered how she was going to stay immune with him looking more tempting than the food he offered.

Chapter Four

Curse watched Mia eat her food, doing her best to ignore him. Her raven hair fell around her in waves. The glossy length tempted him to reach out and touch. She didn't dispute his claim, and he had an idea as to why she was nice to others but kept him at arms' length.

Her palm stayed still on the table, and he wondered what had happened in her past to make her this unapproachable to other men. Whizz had gotten in touch with him while he'd been waiting in the pharmacy for her mother's pills. While he was there, he'd gotten the morning after pill for Mia to take. The pills were effective for up to forty-eight hours after the encounter. Part of him wanted to hand her those pills while another wanted a reason for her to be with him. Ashley and Mia had been best friends even though they'd been different. Where Ashley was the cheerleader getting attention at every turn, Mia was the bookworm. In the yearbook they got voted for the strangest friendship in school.

Whizz had sent him the pictures in an email. Curse read every little detail on his phone as to the mysterious woman before him. Mia was an only child while Ashley had no family to speak of, and on prom night Ashley's father was reported to have left the house and never returned. Ashley reported him as missing after three days from the prom.

There were holes in their lives that even Whizz thought was suspicious. The pictures he saw of Mia showed a happy-go-lucky, kind of girl. She didn't resemble the girl in the picture. This woman in front of him had the weight of the world on her shoulders.

He didn't want to bring up her past tonight. Curse wanted her to relax around him, get used to his company in order for her to confide in him.

She ate her pasta without making a sound.

"This is pretty good," she said, offering a smile.

"I told you I can cook. I'm awesome in the kitchen."

"You certainly look good. I bet more cookbooks would sell with you naked on the front cover." Mia paused with the fork perched in front of her face. "Forget I said anything."

"You think I'm sexy, Mia?" He watched her cheeks heat loving the way they glowed. She bowed her head over her plate, refusing to look at him.

Every chance she got she was always pulling away from him, creating a distance.

"Do you really need me to tell you?" she asked.

"I like hearing you admit it." He stared at her, watching her look at her food, then up at him.

"Well you're going to be waiting around a while. I'm not going to help your ego. It's already big. I'm surprised you can fit into this small kitchen."

He chuckled. Here she went pushing him away.

They finished their food, and he took the dishes, spilling them into the sink. He'd never been the one to do dishes, and he'd arrange for one of the women to clean the place. Grabbing her hand, he lifted Mia out of her seat and led her out of the room.

"Where are we going?"

Curse didn't tell her. He took her upstairs to the main bedroom. Not giving her a chance to dispute him, he pressed her up against the nearest wall. The door was open, and he reached over to slam it shut. Flicking the lock into place, he kept his lips over hers to keep her in place.

She shoved at his chest. The fight in her was pathetic. Mia was fighting him, yet her heart wasn't in it. Sinking fingers into her hair, he moaned at the feel of the soft strands running through his fingers.

Tugging on the length, he bowed her head back, and he kissed down to her neck.

"Tell me to stop, Mia. Tell me this would be rape if I continue." He'd never force a woman who didn't want him. If she really wanted him to stop then he'd do it.

Mia remained silent even as he begged her to tell him to stop. "You want my cock, my hands, my mouth on this fucking body?"

She shook her head.

He worked the top buttons of her uniform open.

"Tell me, Mia, or I'm going to stop this."

"Please, touch me," she said. Her voice was a mere whisper, but she stared at him, unwavering.

"You want my cock?"

Her head jerked in a nod.

"I'm going to need to hear you say it with those pretty lips." He slid his tongue inside her mouth, tasting her.

"Yes."

"Yes, what?"

"I want your cock, your mouth, and your hands." She took hold of his hands and placed his palm over her covered breast. "I want you."

She swallowed past the lump in her mouth. He saw the movement.

Opening the top of her uniform he exposed her chest. The bra she wore was well washed and completely unsexy. He made a mental note to change it when he got the chance. Mia deserved to have sexy underwear that left her feeling more like a woman than anything else.

He shoved the uniform off her shoulders and watched it fall to the floor at her feet. She was curvy in all the right places. Curse put his hands on her hips seeing her flesh against his palm. "You're so sexy and ripe."

She took several indrawn breaths. Watching her inhale, he gazed up her body to rest on her blue eyes. Her skin was pale, her hair was dark, and her eyes the most breathtaking shade of blue. Curse not only saw her beauty, which he was sure many men saw. He saw deeper than that. Her eyes held knowledge of pain. The damage was so clear to see as she stared back at him. Whatever happened in the past had left its mark in her eyes if not on her body. From the front, he saw her skin was flawless, not a mark or a clue as to what she had done in the past.

Releasing her hair, he slid the strap of her bra down her arms. He reached around her, unhooking the strap of her bra to expose her large tits. The nipples were large, round, and made his mouth water.

"Do you want me to stop?"

"No."

He smiled into her eyes. The desperation lingered in her depths. She was so used to controlling every aspect of her life, and here he was, giving her back that control. Did she need for him to not give her a choice anymore?

Cupping her naked breast, he watched her eyes dilate. He tugged at her panties, and they snapped at the harsh tug.

"You keep ruining my underwear."

"I'll buy you nicer ones."

With a hand on her breast, he cupped her pussy, sliding a finger through her slit. She cried out.

"You're so fucking wet. Are you horny, baby?"

"Yes."

Gliding down, he slid a finger into her pussy then a second finger, stretching her.

He pressed a thumb to her clit watching her eyes

close. When he pinched her nipple she jerked in his arms, screaming.

"A little bit of pain goes a long way, baby."

She bit her lip, not disputing him.

Gritting his teeth, he felt her hot cunt grip his finger as he worked them inside her. "This is what you can get from me, Mia. I can give you a nice hard fuck. I can make your body come alive and give you the pleasure that consumes you until I'm the only one you think about."

"And?" she asked.

Curse stared into her eyes, seeing the challenge reflect back at him.

Releasing her pussy and breast, he took a step back leaving some distance between them. He took another step back. Curse shoved his jeans down, exposing his body for her to see. Sitting on the edge of the bed, he stared into her eyes, gripping his cock.

"What are you doing?"

He stroked his length and stared up and down at her naked body. She was so fucking tempting that she made him ache for more.

"You want me, then you've got to come and get me, baby."

She laughed. "What are you trying to prove?"

"Nothing. I'm just curious to see if you'll come and get what you want or if I'll have to come and claim you." He wouldn't move from this spot.

Mia was the type of woman he'd need to catch. She didn't trust anyone around her.

"You're being an asshole."

"Really? You think I'm being an asshole because I'm giving you a choice?"

"What choice?"

He smiled. "Either come here and get fucked by

me or get your clothes and leave."

"I can't leave. I don't even know where we are."

"Then I suggest you make a choice, Mia." He cupped his balls, staring down the length of her body. Her tits were so ripe and full. They rose up and down with each indrawn breath. Her hips were wide, and he couldn't wait to fuck her from behind while grabbing those hips. Did she like her ass being fucked? He wanted to lay claim to her ass, mouth, and cunt. Every part of her was going to know what it was like to be fucked by him.

"There is no choice." She turned away from him, showing off that lush ass.

"Do you really think it's hard to pick me over leaving?" He released his cock. "There's no hiding here, Mia. You don't want to tell me about your past, then fine. I won't ask anymore. You don't want to date, then we don't date. If you want to fuck, then you will come to me."

"Or what?" she asked, gazing at him over her shoulder.

"Or I will fuck up every man you come into contact with. They'll find a line of them waiting at the hospital," he said.

"You'd really do that?"

"Baby, you're mine. The sooner you realize who owns you, the better your life will be."

"I'm my own person."

"I'm not stopping you from being your own person. What I'm saying is you're mine."

He watched her fight. Running a finger across his lip, he waited for her to cave. She was a fiery woman and filled with so much lust. No man had ever gotten her to orgasm. The shock on her face in the bathroom had been clear for him to see. Curse liked the fact he was the only man to bring her to orgasm. He intended to be her first in many aspects of their lives.

****

Curse was such a stubborn bastard. He wouldn't give Mia a chance to leave. She wanted to walk out of that door and make her way home, but she wanted his warmth to surround her. The heat of the night would keep her skin warm, yet inside never felt warm. She didn't know why she always felt empty. Jerry's offer this morning came back to her. What would it be like to have a man to fuck every day?

No, she wouldn't do that. Fucking was not the answer to her problems.

"No commitments."

"None. We fuck. That's it." He stared at her, assessing. Curse always saw more than he should. She hated how easily he read her. She wasn't some *thing* to be read and to know all the answers to. Her life didn't accommodate men or time for herself.

She took a step closer. Curse wasn't looking for commitment. He didn't want anything from her but a fuck. Sex Mia could handle. Anything else and she moved on.

Standing in front of him, she stared down into his face.

"Just sex."

"Who are you trying to convince?" he asked.

Sinking to her knees before him, she stared up at him. "No one. I want to be clear I'm not after anything else."

"Then we'll fuck and nothing else." He sank his fingers into her hair, tugging on the strands. She loved his touch, the bite of pain as he held her in place. Curse didn't apologize for his actions. Mia loved it a little bit rough.

"Does this make me a club whore?" she asked.

His grip tightened. Tears sprang to her eyes at the tight grip, but she didn't tell him to stop. She loved the pain and would be glad for him to go harder.

"No. Club whores fuck every member who wants a fuck. You're not going with anyone but me. The only cock inside you will be mine."

"Will you be fucking other women while you're fucking me?"

"No."

"Monogamy? Are you sure you can handle that?" she asked, teasing him.

He ran his thumb along her lip. "Open."

She opened her lips, and he slid his thumb inside. Sucking his thumb into her mouth, she closed her lips around him, watching his reactions.

"I can handle anything you can throw at me, Mia. I'm not some fucking pussy who'll walk away because I don't like your attitude. You want to fuck, and we'll fuck. If you want to treat me like your own personal dildo then I'll be there. Be warned, Mia, you'll get exactly the same back."

Releasing his thumb, she stared up at him. "What do you mean?"

"I won't have any other woman, and any dildos or sex toys in your possession are now mine. You won't get any cock but mine. You'll become my own little blow up doll. When I want to fuck you, you'll open those legs and let me fuck you." He cupped one of her breasts, pinching the nipple. She cried out. Curse took advantage, claiming her lips, slamming his tongue in deep.

He broke the kiss first, leaving her bereft of his touch.

"You came to me. Why do I have to suffer? You wanted this." She tried to argue with him even as heat spilled between her thighs.

"Only because you kept me at arms' length. I'm not going to be put off anymore. You force everyone away from you, Mia. Not me. I won't be pushed aside."

There was no reason for her to argue, and she kept looking at him.

"Grab my cock."

She couldn't move her head without causing herself pain. Reaching out blindly, she found his cock and started to stroke him. The tip had copious amounts of pre-cum leaking out of the top.

"Fuck."

He placed his fingers over hers and started to work the length together. Curse moved her head, and he pressed the tip of his cock to her lips. "Now, suck it."

Opening her lips, she flicked the tip taking his pre-cum. She moaned and took the tip into her mouth, sucking hard on him.

Curse growled and tugged on her head to take more of him inside her mouth. Mia didn't fight him, taking more and more of his cock into her mouth.

"You know how to suck cock, baby."

She didn't respond. Closing her eyes, she used her mouth and hands on his shaft. With one hand she worked from the root to where her lips met his cock. The other hand she fondled his balls watching the pleasure take him by surprise. She loved seeing the way she blew his mind with her touch alone.

He had control of her head, and she worked to his pace, taking more and more of his cock into her mouth. Her moans were muffled by his cock, but Curse's sounds echoed around the room.

"You're going to be the death of me."

Mia continued to work his cock, taking as much pre-cum from him as she could get. When he no longer wanted her mouth on him, he tugged her up to the bed.

His hands went from her hair to her hips, lowering her down to the bed.

Curse stood over her, gripping his cock as he stared at her.

"What are you doing?" she asked.

"I'm going to play a little. Your body is so fucking beautiful." He followed her down on the bed, lying down one side of her. The intimacy of the act wasn't lost on her, and all she wanted to do was run away from him. To Mia, intimacy was bad. Men wanted to know every little secret from the past. She couldn't give them what they wanted, but she couldn't live life like Ashley. Her friend thrived from all the male attention while she couldn't stand it.

"Where did you go?" he asked, stroking a hand down her body.

"Nowhere."

She fisted her hands at her sides and turned to look at the ceiling.

"You're going to fight me at every turn, aren't you?"

Glancing at him, she saw the amusement in his face.

"Why are you laughing?" she asked.

"I'm not. The next couple of months are going to be so much fun."

She glared at him, folding her arms over her breasts. "We won't last a couple of months."

His hand touched her hip. The smallest touch of his hand and the electricity was instant. Her body was alert to every touch of him.

"Why?" He kissed her shoulder.

"You'll find another woman you want to fuck more."

Curse chuckled. His arm captured her attention.

The ink on his arms was not in any order. He had a picture of a skull and crossbones then interwoven words through some tribal tattoo. There was also a picture of an eagle. None of the ink had any significance that she could see. From the look of each piece of ink, it was as if he discovered something he loved.

"You've got a low opinion of yourself."

"I'm a realist."

"No, you've got your head in the sand, baby. You're blinded by whatever's in here." He touched her temple. "I'm not going anywhere. You'll realize that soon enough."

He slid his fingers down from her head to graze her breasts. She watched those fingers tease her nipples, sliding over one then going to another. Curse glided down to dip into her belly button.

"Don't worry, Mia. I've got a long time to prove to you I'm not going anywhere." Curse opened her thighs and made her open her legs so one was laid over his hips. "There, you're nice and open for me."

Staring into his eyes, she felt a lump in her throat at the smallest of touch.

Curse slid a finger through her slit, teasing her open to his touch. "You're wet for me."

Words failed her. What could she say to him or do? There was nothing. Curse slowly was tearing her apart, and she didn't know how to cope with what he was doing to her.

Two fingers slid to the knuckle inside her followed by a third.

"Your pussy is nice and tight. I love how you grip my cock when I'm inside you."

His thumb stroked over her clit. Fisting her hands at her sides, she forced herself to look at him. Curse wasn't watching what he was doing to her body. He kept his gaze on her face all the time.

He brushed his lips across hers, and she whimpered at the contact. There was nowhere else for her to go. Curse was forcing her to break her icy walls.

"Let go, Mia. Give yourself to me and I promise to take care of you."

She shook her head. No, no one would take care of her or look after her. Mia needed to keep her wits about her.

"Fine. You want to hold yourself back then go ahead." The bed dipped from his body. He moved between her legs, sliding his naked cock against her. "But here you cannot fight me for long."

Within seconds his cock was working inside her. She could find no argument for him. His hands went to her hips, and he slid inside her to the hilt. Crying out, she stared up into his eyes, feeling lost.

"It's okay, baby. You can fight me all you want. I'm not going to back down. You want to be a brick wall then I'll show you how easy they are to knock the fuck down." He pulled out of her body only to slam back inside her.

Pleasure took over, and Mia couldn't find a reason to fight with him. In her heart, the only man she wanted to break down her walls was Curse.

Chapter Five

Mia's cunt gripped him tightly, and Curse stared down into her shocked eyes. She was so beautiful that she stole his heart. There was no other woman for him. His brothers would laugh at the challenge before him. Chaos Bleeds had so many women at their fingertips that they didn't need to go around fighting for a good fuck. Ashley would give him what he wanted without argument.

None of them suited him. He wanted Mia. From the moment he saw her in the diner about to take their order, he'd wanted her. Her hair was darker than Ashley's and her resolve to not get involved absolute. The two women intrigued him, but Mia took his obsession for her to a whole new level.

Taking hold of her hands, he pressed them on either side of her head.

"You're holding me down?"

"I'm in charge. Don't tell me how to fuck you or you're not going to like the answer." Holding her hands down on the bed, he worked into her pussy, watching her gasp and try to hide it. There was so much passion inside her, but she kept it locked up. He was going to work tirelessly to open her up for him and him alone. "Wrap your legs around my waist."

She circled her legs around his hips, and he fucked her hard, plunging in deep. Mia cried out first, the sounds echoing around the room as she gave into his plunges. He intended to have her screaming for the rest of the night. Her voice was going to be hoarse from the work.

Curse took her roughly, fucking her to the hilt and holding her down. Her tits bounced with each of his thrusts, but still he didn't stop. Slamming his lips down on hers, he swallowed down her cries, loving the feel of her cunt wrapped around his shaft.

Releasing one of her hands, he slid down and started to stroke her clit. The rippling in her pussy got harder as he worked her pussy. Kissing her neck, he sucked on the pulse beating rapidly against her flesh.

"Come on, Mia, come all over my cock. Show me how fucking dirty you can get. I want to feel every drop of cum soaking my length."

She groaned and jerked in his arms. He pinched her clit and slammed inside her then stroked the hurt away throwing Mia into orgasm. Her cum washed all over his cock. Groaning, he slammed in deep while also caressing her clit.

"Stop, please, stop, no more." She screamed the words after he continued to caress her clit.

Curse stopped stroking her body and pulled out of her heat.

"What are you doing?" she asked. Her gaze moved to his.

"Get on your knees."

Mia hesitated for several seconds before going to her knees before him. He stared at the expanse of her ass. She was so fucking sexy. His cock was wet with her cream.

Spreading the cheeks of her ass open, he stared at the entrance of her cunt. Her cum leaked out and dripped down to her clit.

Looking at the puckered hole of her ass, he was tempted to fuck her there.

"You ever been taken in the ass?"

"No."

That was going to be something he remedied.

Sliding his cock through her slit, he bumped her nub then dropped back to plunge into her. Gripping her hips, he groaned from the new depth of her pussy. She squeezed him tight. Her juices eased his path all the way inside her.

"Do you feel me, baby?"

"Yes."

"Your pussy better get used to me being inside you. I'm never going to stop." He rammed inside her to the hilt, loving each gasp and ripple coming from her.

For several thrusts, he held onto her hips and simply fucked her loving the feel of how deeply he plunged inside her from this angle. Gazing down at her ass, the temptation to play with her was too strong. Releasing one hip, he slid his fingers through her cream, stroking her clit in the process. Her screams were muffled by the pillow underneath her.

He slapped her ass, and she jerked looking around at him.

"Those screams are mine. Make sure I can fucking hear them." He slapped her ass again for good measure.

She threw the pillow away from her, and he got to hear every moan without it being muffled from the fabric.

Coating his fingers with her natural lube, he pressed his fingers to the puckered hole of her ass. Mia froze.

"This is mine now, baby. No fighting me."

"I don't want you to fuck my ass."

"I won't fuck your ass tonight, but I'll get you ready to fuck it when I want." Thrusting inside her, he caressed over her ass waiting for her to relax. She didn't give in to him. Mia stayed tense, but he wasn't having any of it. Working her cunt and ass together he slowly gave her no choice but to relax.

When she was no longer tense, he pressed the tip

of one finger to her ass. He eased past the tight ring of muscles determined to keep him out. She tensed a little but no longer enough to give her pain.

He paused inside her pussy as he slowly eased one finger inside her anus. She shook beneath him. Curse held her hip as he worked the finger into the knuckle. He took his time, making sure she accepted him into her body with ease.

After several seconds passed, he added in a second finger.

"No more," she said, tightening around him. He had no intention of pushing her too far with her first time. Pumping into her ass, he worked his fingers into her ass feeling her come apart. Her pussy constantly clenched around him, and her cream spilled over his arousal.

"You love the feel of my cock, don't you, baby?"

"Yes."

"You're going to give me this cunt every chance I get." He didn't pose it as a question, but still she answered it.

"Yes."

Over and over, he plundered her warmth while also working her ass. She started to thrust back against him. Curse didn't mind her getting involved.

The only sound in the room was that of their heavy breathing. He had her naked, taking his cock and hands, and he wasn't going to complain.

"Fuck me, baby. Show me how fucking hot you are."

Ramming inside her, Curse felt the first stirrings of his orgasm start. One final thrust and he growled his release. Even through the haze of pleasure, he wanted Mia to come. No longer gripping her hip, he teased her clit. Within seconds she was coming right along with him.

Collapsing over her, he removed his fingers from her ass but stayed within her tight pussy.

"Do you have any diseases?" she asked.

"No."

"I'm going to get on the pill or do something." Her body vibrated from the words she spoke. Curse wrapped an arm around her body. He'd carry her through to the bathroom when he was ready.

His body was too weak to move.

"Why?"

"I don't want kids, Curse. Sex with you is going to end up with kids if you're not prepared to wear protection."

After feeling her once without a condom, Curse didn't want to spoil the fun. She'd never believe him, but she was the first woman he'd ever taken without the use of a rubber.

"Whatever. You're not taking the morning after pill. What happens, happens."

"If I'm pregnant I'm not keeping it."

He turned her over, glaring down at her. "You're not killing anything we make together. If there's a baby, I'll be a fucking father to it."

"You couldn't father a fucking child, Curse. You're out on the road more often than not. Ashley told me you can't stand to be grounded for long. Newsflash, babies need constant attention."

His anger spiked. Pulling out of her body, he stared down at her fisting his hands at his sides.

"I'm going to wash up. You better consider what you've just said by the time I get back."

"Why?" she asked, arms folded over her breasts.

"Because I don't make it a habit to hurt a woman. You talk that shit again I may make an exception." He stormed off, letting his words sink in. Curse knew he wouldn't hurt her, but Mia didn't have the first fucking clue as to what she said.

No, he didn't stay home for long periods of time. Each time he left Piston County he had a pretty good reason. The Skulls were attracted to trouble. Devil wouldn't leave his friend to suffer. Chaos Bleeds and The Skulls had a precarious relationship but one that worked.

If he had a woman and a kid then he wouldn't be rushing off whenever trouble lurked around the corner.

Washing his cock and fingers, he returned to the bedroom with a cloth.

"I'm sorry," she said. "It was rude of me to say something so awful. I don't know how you'd be as a father for your child."

Staring at her, he nodded, accepting her apology.

Mia was an enigma. On the one hand she was a bitch, fighting him at every turn, but then she turned and was this sweet woman who looked totally lost.

When he got a chance to, he was going to fucking give some to Ashley. The other woman was accepted by the club, but that didn't mean she had the right to tell Mia about his business.

****

Mia woke to strong, ink covered arms wrapped around her. Glancing behind her she saw Curse was asleep holding onto her tightly. There was no chance of leaving his side without him waking up. Blowing some hair off her face, she stayed in his arms, trying her hardest not to tense.

"You want to fuck, little girl. I can give you what you want."

The words haunted her, and on the clock beside the bed she saw it was the anniversary of what she had done. Closing her eyes, she counted to ten to stop herself from thinking about *him*.

"Stop being tense. It's the morning, and you've just woken up. No one should be this tense." Curse muttered the words against her ear and kissed her neck.

"I've got to go." She didn't have cleaning today for other people. Mia worked a double shift at the diner doing the morning then the afternoon shift.

"Where?"

"I've got to work."

"Again."

"Real people have to deal with real work." Mia kept facing the wall.

"What? You don't think I work? I work fucking hard. Devil has us working at the club, the strip club, and doing whatever we need to do for Jerry."

The mention of Jerry made her tense. He noticed.

"How the fuck do you know Jerry?"

"I used to clean his house." She tried to climb out of the bed, but Curse wasn't letting her go.

"There's more to it than that. Used to, why did you stop?"

"It's none of your business. I need to pee. Will you let me the fuck go?"

"No, stay still and answer my fucking question."

Growling in frustration, she turned to glare at him.

"What part of it being none of your business don't you get?"

"You know what he is. I want to know why you tensed up at the mention of his name. I'm not fucking stupid, Mia. Tell me."

Throwing her arms up in the air, she didn't see him letting her get away with anything. "He offered me a job yesterday. A working job with male clients. Can you believe two men within hours of each other offering me money to fuck them? Get off me." She shoved his arm away, shocked he let her go.

"You're not working for him again."

"Duh, I stopped it instantly. I told him to get another cleaner. I'm not for sale." Storming into the bathroom, she did her business, washed her hands then brushed her teeth with the spare toothbrush. Entering the bedroom she saw Curse was stretching to his full height.

Words failed her as she looked at him. Every single hard muscle was on display for her to see.

"Do you want to come and lick me? You've got drool coming from your mouth already."

Sticking her tongue out, she grabbed her uniform and started to wriggle into the dress. With the dress on her hips, she fixed her bra into place.

"You work too much," he said.

"I work enough to make my mom comfortable. Most people would do the same."

"No they wouldn't. A lot of people are self-centered assholes who couldn't give a fuck about their parents. You're different. Angel would like you."

She turned to him. "Who is Angel?"

He chuckled. "Are you jealous?"

"No, of course not." The lies came easily as he finished buttoning up her dress.

"Angel is one of the women at The Skulls. Lash's woman who seems to attract as much trouble as the club itself. She's a sweetheart and loves Lash."

"You sound in love with her."

"Nah, she's too sweet for me. I like a woman who's not afraid to show me her claws."

Mia rolled her eyes. "I need you to take me to the diner. I'm not going to get home to take care of my mom. Will you do that for me?"

"Sure, for a price."

Shoulders dropping, she stared at him. "What do you want?"

"A kiss."

"What?"

"I'll go and check on your mother and all you've got to do is put those pretty lips on mine."

As she stared at him for several seconds, he didn't move away. They faced each other, and she was struck by how different they were.

"A kiss for you to check on my mom. You spent all night kissing and fucking me."

"Exactly, I want to know what it's like to have those beautiful lips on mine without me having to take charge." He stepped closer, invading her space.

"You're making me do it now."

"Maybe I am, but you're going to have to convince me that you want this or I won't go and help your mother."

She wanted to deny him. Her break was more than enough time for her to get back to her mother.

Kiss him. You know you want to.

Running her hands up his bare chest, she circled her hands around his neck. "Curse, would you look after my mother?"

Before he could answer, she tugged him down to kiss him. He didn't fight her and came down to her easily. She slid her tongue over his lips, and he opened his to let her inside.

Playing with the hair at the base of his neck, she melted against him loving the feel of his lips on hers.

His hand caught her ass, and Curse took over, kissing her deeply.

After what felt like a lifetime she pulled away from him. He licked his lips and smiled.

"Baby, you didn't really have to convince me. I was happy with a kiss on the cheek."

She punched him in the arm.

A quick breakfast of coffee and toast, and they were out on his bike. She held onto Curse as he rode the way back to the diner. He'd given her a pair of boxers to wear in place of the panties he tore the night before.

Outside of the diner he kept the bike running.

"I'll come and collect you tonight."

"I can't stay away from my mom two nights in a row."

"I'm not asking you to. We'll spend the night at your mother's. Don't worry, I won't fuck you for her to hear even though I think she'd be happy to know you get some excitement."

She slapped his shoulder again. "Stop it. Make sure she takes her medication."

Turning her back on him, she walked into the diner aware of his gaze on her. Mia saw she still had thirty minutes before her actual shift began. Nodding at several of the customers and waitresses she made her way to the staff room. Sitting on the bench nearest her locker she thought over what happened last night.

He was never going to let up. Curse didn't fool her. The questions would stop for her, but he wouldn't stop in his attempt to find out the answers. The staff room had a phone for them to make calls. She placed a couple of cents in the bowl and dialed Ashley's number.

It rang a couple of times before Ashley answered.

"Whoever the fuck that is you tell them to be reasonable next time." A male was shouting in the background.

"Shut it, Pussy. It's my phone, and I can have calls whenever the hell I want. Hello," Ashley said.

"Hey, it's me, Mia."

"Mia, honey, how are you?"

"Check the date. How do you think I am?"

The silence on the other end was deafening.

"Hey, where are you going?" Pussy asked.

"I've got to take this in private." Ashley spoke up.

Resting her head against the wall, Mia wished she hadn't called, but the only person she could talk to was her friend.

"I'm outside now. No one can hear us. What's the matter, Mia?" Ashley asked.

"I just, I don't know. I needed to talk to you. You're the only one I can trust."

"It was a long time ago. Prom night, remember. We promised each other we wouldn't do this. We covered our asses, so stop bringing it up before you fucking curse us." Ashley sounded broken over the line.

"I can't stop." Taking deep breaths, Mia did her best to get her rioting emotions under control. "It's all right for you. You didn't do anything."

"I was there, and I helped. He was a bastard, Mia. We did the right thing."

"You mean I did."

"Is this about Curse? Is he asking questions?" Ashley asked.

"He's always asking questions. It's only a matter of time before he finds out the truth." Opening her eyes, she turned to face the room. "He won't take no for an answer." And she'd grown tired of fighting him. She was always fighting him, and it hurt at times.

"Then make him forget about your past."

"There's only so much I can do and say. He's relentless."

Ashley started talking about other things.

"I need you to sleep with him," Mia said, cutting

her friend off.

"What?"

"He promised there wouldn't be any other women. If you sleep with him, it's a reason for me to stop."

Silence met her answer.

"Mia, I'm not some whore to use like that."

"You've fucked him before, and you sleep with half the club. I'm not offering you cash. I've got none. I need you to help me to stop him from wanting to be with me."

Ashley hysterical chuckle came over the line.

"You're not going to help me?" Mia asked, angry.

"I can't help you with this."

"You asked me to keep this a secret. I've done everything in my power to make your life easier, Ashley. Help me with this, or I swear to God, you and I will no longer have anything in common as I'll turn myself in." She slammed the phone down.

Mia wasn't lying. She was tired of feeling this way, and if the only way to make it all stop was to come clean, then she would.

Chapter Six

Curse stormed into the clubhouse within half an hour of dropping Mia off. He went straight for the office where he knew Devil would be. Entering the office he found his president on the phone looking serious.

"You're fucking serious? Alex did it? Shit, Tiny, what are you going to do?"

Devil looked up at him and nodded for him to take a seat.

"Butch is not going to come back to The Skulls now."

Tiny was obviously saying something else.

"I know, and Angel is settling in again?"

"She's still in Italy with Lash?"

His president nodded. The conversation was one sided. Tapping his leg, Curse waited for the phone call to end. Ten minutes later Devil hung up. "I'm telling you we settled in the wrong fucking town. Tiny and The Skulls are dealing with a whole load of other drama."

"Who with?" Curse asked.

"Butch and Alex." Devil shook his head. "I'm not going to get into it. It's fucking ridiculous, but I'm sure we'll be dragged back to Fort Wills in no time. Lexie has agreed to go. Eva's arranging a family barbeque for all of us to be invited. It will be good. Anyway, why are you here?"

"I want to kill Jerry."

The other man burst out laughing. "Yeah, right, it's not going to happen."

"I'm being fucking serious. I want to kill Jerry, and I want permission off you to do it." Curse's words sobered Devil up.

"Okay, why do you want to kill the man we're in business with?" Devil asked, leaning back in his chair.

"He offered my woman a job as a call girl."

"Mia, the woman from the diner."

Curse frowned. "How do you know about her?"

"It doesn't take a fucking genius to realize shit like this. Also, I know everything about my men." Devil shook his head. "We're not going to start something with Jerry. He offered your woman a job, but that doesn't mean he was being disrespectful to you."

"What would you do if it was Lexie?" Curse asked, knowing he hit below the belt.

"Come on, let's go and deal with this shit." Devil got to his feet, grabbing his keys from the desk. He flipped his cell phone open and dialed a number. "Hey, babe. Did you sleep well this morning?"

Tuning out of the one sided conversation Curse spotted Ashley in the corner of the clubhouse looking pale. He frowned but didn't stop to say hi. Curse would deal with her when he got back.

"Oh, where are we going?" Pussy asked, joining them.

"I'm going to kill Jerry."

"Sounds exciting. I'm coming along."

Pussy joined them, and Devil walked out of the clubhouse five minutes later. Straddling his bike, he followed Devil out of the compound. He hoped Jerry was at home. The desire to sink his fist into the guy's face was strong.

The roads were not that busy as they drove up the main road. Outside of Jerry's house a woman was struggling with four large suitcases.

"Aren't you going to help me?" she asked, screaming at Jerry.

"You want me to help you leave me? You've got no chance, baby. You want to leave, do it under you own steam."

Curse smirked even though he wanted to hate the bastard. Jerry was a pimp, a drug dealer and the owner of respectable companies, but he loved the rounded woman struggling to put the cases in her cheap ass car. The other man looked annoyed. His two kids were buckled into their seats as they passed the car.

Jerry nodded at Devil. "I'll be with you in a second once my wife decides if she's leaving or not."

"I'm leaving. I am fucking leaving you." She threw curses at Jerry, hatful words even. Curse saw through it all. The woman was in pain, and she was doing everything she could to force herself to leave.

After ten minutes, Jerry was on his cell phone. A limousine pulled up outside of the house. Curse watched as he carried his two kids to the waiting limo then went to his wife. When they first met Jerry, he was married to a blonde, slender woman who was a viperous bitch. Melanie had been his mistress. Within the few years of them being in Piston County, the wife had gone and Melanie became his wife. The drama hadn't all been there.

"I hate you," she said.

"I know, and I promise you nothing happened."

She shook her head. Jerry placed her in the back of the limo and told the driver where to take them.

Once the limo was out of the street, Jerry turned back to them.

"Sorry about that." The other man looked lost.

"Trouble in paradise?" Devil asked. His president had been there for the wedding.

"You could say that. She's under the impression I've got a mistress hiding somewhere because of what I did with her." He picked up two of her cases with ease. "She trashed the house the other day in our argument, and now she wants a divorce."

Curse grabbed the other two cases, and together they entered the house.

"Do you have a mistress?" Devil asked.

Since they settled down, Devil had turned into a gossip.

"No, I've not. Fuck, having Melanie as my mistress was a fucking mistake. I saw her when I was away from home and fell for her, but I was married to that fucking viper." Jerry shook his head. "She'll soon come around."

"If not, you've got another divorce on your hands," Pussy said, sounding cheery.

"Great, thank you. Why are you here?"

"Curse wants to kill you," Devil said, taking a seat in the nearest sofa. "You propositioned his woman, and he's come to hurt you for it."

Jerry frowned. "Seriously? A whore convinced you she wasn't a whore."

"Mia's no whore."

The other man tensed then cursed.

"I had no idea she was taken." Jerry moved over to the bottles of scotch. "It's five o'clock somewhere, and I've had enough already."

"Why did you offer her a job as an escort?" Curse asked.

"I offered her a chance to make extra money. She works two jobs, and in case any of you are blind, she's a fucking stunner. The raven hair, pale skin, and fucking ocean eyes will earn her a fucking fortune." Jerry took a long swallow of his drink. "I may be married, but I also know how to make fucking money. She's struggling, and she doesn't have to."

"You weren't going to test out the goods for yourself?" Curse glared at the other man, knowing the fight was leaving him.

"No. Regardless of what others think I'm satisfied with my wife. There are men out there who'd pay for a night with Mia, and she wouldn't be laboring away for a pittance either. She's yours, fine. I didn't mean to overstep the line."

Turning to Devil, who was smiling, Curse shook his head. "I won't be killing anyone today."

"See, we can get through life without killing everything." Devil got to his feet. "Good luck with your woman."

"Thanks. It's going to take more than luck to get me what I want," Jerry said. "You guys know where the front door is."

"Wow, that was rather anti-climactic," Pussy said. They were outside where several schoolgirls passed them, giggling.

All three men sneered at them. None of them were into young girls in the bedroom.

"He was trying to help my woman, not sleep with her. I can't kill him for that. She works too damn hard."

Straddling his bike, Curse looked at the other two men.

"Is she going to be your old lady?" Devil asked.

"I don't know. She won't be honest with me, but I'll let you know the moment I do."

"Once she is, she'll be under the club protection," Devil said. "I'm going home to my woman and kids. See you guys later."

Heading back to the clubhouse, Curse parked his car up and made a note to go sort out Mia's mother. He needed a wash and a change of clothes.

Going to his room, he paused when he found Ashley sat outside of his door on the floor. Her feet were up to her chest as she stared into space. Clearing his throat, he got her attention. Her eyes were red from crying.

"What's going on?" he asked.

"Nothing, I thought it would be nice for us to catch up. It has been a long time since we got to know each other."

Entering his room, he let Ashley enter. The sound of the lock flicking into place had him turning toward her. She was swigging from a bottle of scotch.

"What are you doing? We're not going to be fucking. Pussy is downstairs. Give him some attention. I don't want it."

She moved to his side, running a hand down his chest, similar to the way Mia had done hours ago.

Catching her wrist, he stopped her from going down any further. "I said no."

"Come on, Curse, you know how much you love to fuck me?"

He frowned, staring at her. She wouldn't meet his eyes, and he grew suspicious. Ashley was a sweet woman even with her preference for sex.

"What's going on?" he asked.

"Nothing. I just miss your cock. You know how big you are."

"I also know Pussy is bigger, and you like him a little more." Folding his arms, he took a step back. This was a puzzle, and he liked figuring out puzzles. Her hand shook as she raised the bottle to her lips. "Why are you drinking this early?"

"It's good to start drinking early. The party is going to start soon enough." She turned away from him, and he watched her wipe something from under her eye.

"Are you crying?"

"No, I'm not crying. Why won't you fuck me?" she asked, snapping at him.

"Watch how you fucking speak to me."

He stared at her and wondered what the fuck was going on. Why she was here didn't make any sense to him.

"I'm with Mia now. There will be no fucking around."

"Mia won't mind."

She stared somewhere past his shoulder.

Grabbing her arms, he glared at her. "You better tell me what the fuck is going on right now, or I swear I will make your life a fucking misery."

Ashley sobbed seconds before collapsing against him. When she told him the truth, his anger spiked. Mia was going to know not to fucking mess with him.

****

Tired, fed up, and angry at herself, Mia entered the staff room to grab her bag. Resting her head against the wall, she cursed herself for her actions earlier. Since hanging up the phone, she'd regretted her words to Ashley. She didn't want Ashley to sleep with Curse or to have anything to do with him. Rubbing at her chest, she took several deep breaths to try to calm her nerves.

Will he sleep with her?

The thought of his hard body moving over Ashley filled her with jealousy. She heard several women giggling as they looked over a magazine. Ignoring them, she grabbed her bag and headed out the front door. Curse waited for her with his arms folded. He was staring at the ground rather than at her. Walking across the road, she stopped in front of him.

"Hey," she said.

He looked up, and she saw the anger lurking in his eyes. Pausing a step away from him, she fisted her palms.

"What's the matter?" she asked.

"I could ask you the same question."

"I don't know what you're talking about." She looked at the ground without meeting his gaze.

Curse reached out, grasping her chin in his hand. "Don't fucking lie to me. Get on the bike."

"We're going home to my mom, right?"

"She's being well taken care of. I put Pussy and Ashley onto her care."

"What? She can't be around a total stranger."

"Which is why I sent Ashley with him. Don't worry, nothing bad will happen to your mom. Now, get on the back of the fucking bike before I lose it here for all of them to see."

Teeth gritted, she looped her arm through her backpack and moved toward his bike. She didn't see any reason to argue.

He gunned the engine and took off out of town. She wasn't too concerned with the direction of where they were going. Curse wouldn't hurt her regardless of what others thought.

Keeping her arms banded around his waist, she held onto him as the wind blew through her hair. Closing her eyes, she tried to think of the reason as to why he was so angry with her. Nothing made any sense, not his anger, unless he knew about Ashley. *Crap.* What if her friend had spilled the beans on her? Several minutes later, Curse pulled up outside of the house they'd stayed in the night before. He waited for her to climb off, then took hold of her hand, leading her into the house. The moment the door was shut her back was pressed to the wall.

"Who the fuck do you think you are?" Curse asked. His face was red with rage.

"What?"

"Do you really think I'd sleep with Ashley if she came onto me like a cheap fucking whore?"

Shame consumed her at what she'd done. "Listen—"

"No, you fucking listen." His palm smacked against the wall the other side of her head. She jerked from the harshness of the movement. Curse's anger took her completely by surprise. It changed him, made him scarier than she ever imagined.

"You really thought I wouldn't find out about what you'd done?" he asked.

"I didn't think about you when I asked her to do what I wanted. I only thought about getting you off my back."

He shook his head. "You're a real piece of work, do you know that?"

His words hurt, but Mia knew she deserved him lashing out.

She shook her head, tears filling her eyes.

"God, I can't believe this. You know, there are thousands of women out there who'd be begging for my attention. Instead, I've got to try to convince you that I want to be here," he said.

Running shaky fingers through her hair, she stared up at him. "I'm sorry," she said.

"It's not good enough. Not from you. I deserve something far better from you."

"Look, I made a mistake. I realize that."

Curse held his hands up stopping her from talking. "No. You told Ashley to fuck me so you'd have a reason to leave me. It's not going to happen."

Both of his hands rested on the wall on either side of her.

"What are you doing?" she asked.

"I'm keeping my hands where I can see them before I do something I regret like hurt you."

Scared, Mia stared at his chest. "I'm sorry."

"Shut the fuck up."

Nodding, she ran her fingers through her hair for something to do. She squealed as he grabbed her hand and placed then against the wall underneath his large hands.

"Some things are going to change around here, Mia," he said.

"What do you mean?" She tried to keep her voice quiet so she wouldn't anger him.

"From now on, you're going to learn to accept me in your life. This is not going to be about sex or you trying to find some other woman to lure me away." He covered her mouth with his palm as she went to argue with him. "No, shut the fuck up, you little bitch, before I seriously lose my temper."

Mia couldn't believe what he just called her.

You deserve it. You deserve everything he has to say and throw at you.

Licking her lips, she dropped her gaze from his.

"You're going to learn to shut up and to stop arguing with me. I'm not going to deal with your crap. You ever force or even fucking tell another woman to sleep with me then I'll have your fucking hide." He cupped her check.

For some bizarre reason she wasn't afraid of him even though he'd shouted threats to her.

"This is not what I want."

"Your pussy is wet for me," he said.

"It means nothing."

His eye brow rose as he looked at her. "You really think it means nothing?"

"Yes."

She was lying. How could she not be lying? The feelings he inspired from the lust to the jealousy were not easily explained. Mia couldn't deny what was happening to her even if she didn't want it to be true.

"What's so wrong with being with me?" he asked.

"You're a biker."

"And you're talking bullshit."

"You don't know a thing about me or what I'm capable of," she said, blurting the words out. Her dirty past threatened to spill out of her mouth at any moment. The secrets she kept were not for others to know. When Ashley was ready for others to know the truth about what happened to her then she'd come clean about her part. "Forget I ever said anything."

She made to move around him, but he wouldn't let her go. His hand went to her cheek and stayed there.

"No, you don't get to leave." His body trapped her. There was nowhere for her to hide. He was forcing her to face him. "Everyone has a past. Shit, I know some guys who've got so much of a past it gets other people killed."

His voice shouldn't soothe her or make her feel better.

"Fine, you don't want to tell me then I'll never know the answer. I've lived without explanations before, but I swear to you, Mia, you ever try to do that shit again, and me and you are going to have some serious fucking problems."

He shoved away from her, heading toward the kitchen.

"Have you ever killed someone?" she asked.

Curse stopped and turned to look at her.

"You'll have your secrets, and I'll have mine." This time he didn't stop until he was out of sight.

She watched him go feeling like the worst bitch in the world. Walking down to the kitchen, she saw him grabbing stuff from the fridge. "Can I use your phone to call Ashley?"

"Sure." He tossed the cell phone her way and left her to make the call.

Entering the sitting room, she typed in Ashley's number.

"Hey, everything is covered here. Do you have Mia?" Ashley asked.

"It's Mia. I'm with Curse, and everything is fine. I want to phone, to apologize for the shit I said." Pressing a hand to her face, Mia was swamped by the humiliation of what had happened. The things she'd said were completely shameful. "I can't believe I said what I said and did what I did. I'm sorry."

"I love you, Mia. I'll do whatever you need me to do. I owe you so much. You know that, right?"

Shaking her head, Mia pressed a palm to her mouth. "I think I'm going crazy."

"We'll have a girly night soon, and we'll deal with whatever you're going through."

Nodding, at that time she'd agree to anything. Minutes passed, and when they were both feeling better, Mia hung up the call and stared in front of her.

She was losing her mind. Every year it was getting harder, but there was nothing she could do about it. The secret she held within her would be carried to her grave.

Chapter Seven

For the next week Curse divided his time among Mia, her mother, and the club. Ripper was organizing a party for Judi at the clubhouse while Devil was dealing with his family. The whole club was settling into stationary life. The open road was no longer a factor in their life. They all loved to ride, and there were nights when they all took to the road just to clear their head.

Most of the time, Curse was too busy trying to get through to Mia when he wasn't fucking her. He could spend hours inside her tight cunt, licking her pussy, or preparing her ass, but the moment he tried to talk about anything more, she cut him off.

On the one hand it was refreshing to have a woman keep him at arms' length, but on the other, he was getting pissed with fighting her. Mia was a challenge he didn't want to have to deal with.

He saw the yearning in her eyes whenever she looked at him. Curse also saw when she pulled away from him, shutting down. Running fingers through his hair, he grabbed a wrench from the tool box and started to work on his bike. He liked using his hands, and working on his bike was much better than working on his car. Pussy came to stand beside him.

"What's going on with you?" Pussy asked.

"Nothing. Why?" He didn't bother to look at the other man. His attention was on his bike.

"Because you used to help me keep Ashley occupied in the sack, and now you don't go near her. You don't help Vincent, and none of the other club whores have been in your bed in a while. I'm curious. What gives? Is Mia the one? I know you were pissed at Jerry, but you've not made a claim on her or even brought her to the club?"

Standing up, Curse wiped the sweat from his brow with the back of his sleeve. "I'm seeing someone. Yes, it's Mia, but she's not like any other woman I know. The club whores and Ashley don't bother me anymore. I've got what I need in one package. Now, trying to convince my woman of that is fucking hard."

"So, you're really serious about the waitress? The ice-queen who'll freeze your cock off before you get anywhere near her?" Pussy looked positively upset. "Seriously? You're giving up all of our women for *her*."

"I like her. She's what I want, so be careful what you say. I'll still kick your ass if you say anything to fucking insult her."

"What could I say that isn't the truth? She's cold." Pussy shivered and glanced over his shoulder. "She's nothing like Ashley."

Curse checked to see what he was looking at. Ashley was talking with Death and Ripper. The young woman was laughing as if she didn't have a care in the world. He didn't believe any of it.

"She fucks everything that walks."

"Within the club. I bag my shit and don't want a bitch getting too emotionally attached. I'm not up to that kind of crap." Pussy shrugged. "I don't know what you see in the waitress. I bet her cunt will freeze your dick off."

Curse laughed at his friend. Pussy had no idea how she looked after his cock was inside her warm cunt.

"God, that smile. You make me sick." Pussy looked away.

Ashley was approaching them with a wide smile on her lips. "Hey, Curse."

"Hey." He stared at his bike wishing for the peace he had seconds before.

She ran her hand up Pussy's chest, practically

purring as if she was some fucking cat.

"I'm hungry and horny."

"What do you want to eat? I can fix you something," Pussy said, to which Ashley wrinkled her nose.

"You've got no chance. You can't cook. I'd be better off eating cardboard than what you eat. Let's head to the diner. I'm in a serious need for grease, and their burgers are just what I need."

Watching the two people together, Curse saw the friendship between them and nothing else. Ashley was never going to be the settling down kind of girl. She would probably always be a respected club whore who kept the other women in their place.

"Did you hear that Devil is planning on taking on some prospects? Death was telling me about a few of the hangers-on at parties are requesting to join." Ashley shoved some hair off her shoulder. There was a time he thought her black hair was natural like Mia's, and he later learned she got all of her looks out of a box.

"No, I hadn't heard," Curse said. Pussy muttered the same as him. There hadn't been a club meeting for a few months. With Devil's latest son being born, no one expected to be around the club twenty-four seven.

"I don't know. It's just something the other guys were talking about. Are you coming to the diner?" she asked.

"Mia won't be there."

"I know. She's put in a good word for us to one of the other servers." Ashley gripped his arm, holding it close to her breast.

His cock stayed flaccid at the contact. Ashely did nothing for him, not even her body, which was slightly slenderer than Mia's curves.

"Then I'll come. I'm famished." Mia had kept

him up all night with her tight pussy.

Wiping his hands on a cloth, he checked to make sure he fit everything back to his bike and straddled the machine. Ashley climbed on the back of Pussy's and wrapped her arms around his waist. No woman was allowed on the back of Curse's bike. He only had room for one woman, and Mia wasn't going to be moved off his bike ever. She was an addiction that was much better than drugs or booze. Curse knew. He'd tried both kinds of addiction. None of them had really stuck with him. Yeah, he liked a good drink, but losing himself in drugs hadn't been his thing. He liked to keep his wits about him, which drugs didn't offer. Coke, heroin, weed, none of it gave him a buzz like being on the back of his bike.

He knew others in the club did have an addiction, but under Devil's orders, they kept their shit contained. Any man who let the drugs control him ended up six feet under. There was only so much room within the club for that kind of shit. Chaos Bleeds were lenient compared to The Skulls, but even Devil only liked men he could trust around him. Having some prospects around could be useful. The only problem with that was trying to find new brothers was always a challenge. They would have to tests the guys' loyalties, throw crazy assed shit at them with the hope of them figuring it out.

If they had someone who'd tattle at the first opportunity then they were not the kind of men they wanted in their club. It was a brotherhood, a bond, a union, whatever shit people wanted to call them. They had each other's backs, and those who didn't, were gone. There was no room for mistakes in their lives. It was either fight all the way, or die trying. It was one of the reasons why The Skulls had his respect. They would all die for each other, but also, they'd fight to the death for one another.

Entering the diner, Curse noticed the place was crowded. They took the last table at the back of the diner, and a slim blonde headed straight toward them. "Hi, I'm Sandra, and I'll be your server today."

Mia had done this for them. Whenever she wasn't working, she'd fixed to have someone to serve them. He was oddly touched by her actions. Every chance she got, she tried to keep him at arms' length, yet here she was, taking care of him and the club.

They ordered a shitload of food, and Curse relaxed against the plush cushion taking in his surroundings.

He noticed a brunette sitting at a table with some stern looking parents who were glaring at their table. Raising a brow, he kept the man's gaze, waiting to see who'd look away first. The guy looked down at his plate.

Curse noticed him grip the girl's jean covered thigh, tightly. Her cry was silent as her mouth opened, but no sound came out. Staring at the scene Curse took note of the glistening tears in her eyes, but they wouldn't fall down her cheeks. She picked up her fork and continued to eat.

The father removed his hand and smiled over at his wife. The older woman looked at him adoringly.

"Who's that?" he asked, turning to look at Ashley.

She checked to where he pointed with his cup. The sneer on her face was not hard to make out. "Mr. and Mrs. Carmichael. They're snobs of the highest order. Their daughter, Sasha, is a dear, but she's not allowed out of their sight. He's her stepfather and a fucking bastard to boot."

"There's certainly no love lost between the two."

"He causes problems for everyone he doesn't like, and I mean everyone." Ashley looked over the table and glared at him. "He pulled Sasha out of school and wouldn't let her mingle with us low earners."

The control in the other man was absolute. He ordered what his family would eat, and if either of them spoke when he wasn't ready to listen, he cut them down. Curse watched the byplay with the family. Sasha certainly hated him.

Their food came from Sandra, and his thoughts returned to Mia. He wondered what she was like when her father was around to take away some of the slack. There had to be a time when she was happier, easier, more carefree.

Even as he thought it, Curse doubted it. Whatever happened in Mia and Ashley's past would stay there, but it had changed Mia completely.

****

Mia gritted her teeth as Dale got her to bend over the bed to finish smoothing out the covers. She hated this job more than any other. He had her cleaning his office, the kitchen, the sitting room and finally the bathroom downstairs before he ordered her to clean upstairs.

Think about the money.

When she thought about money and the chance of getting her mother's prescription and maybe some meat for dinner, she was able to do what he wanted without even gritting her teeth. It was hard to work for a guy who gave her the creeps.

Since she quit working for Jerry she had more time free to clean. Jerry offered to let the street know of her services, but the only person to take more of her time was Dale, the creep.

"Very nice," he said.

Rolling her eyes, she wondered if she should just tell Curse to have a word with Dale. The thought of that happening filled her with joy. Dale would soon back off with that threat. Climbing off the bed, she was startled as an arm banded around her waist.

"I've got you, baby."

His voice sent chills down her spine. Tugging out of his hold, she tensed as he seemed to grip her a little tighter. Walking around the bed, she saw the time was a little after lunch.

Curse was a creature of habit. She wondered what he was doing for lunch. Earlier in the week she'd spoken to Sandra about serving the table. The other woman had two kids, and her husband was off work with a bad back. Mia told Ashley to advise the men to tip the woman greatly. The extra money would help Sandra out no end. Ashley had argued with her, telling her the men would rather tip her for her mother's medicine, at which point, Mia told her friend she could no longer accept money from them. Curse, in a strange kind of way, was her boyfriend. It was strange for her as she wouldn't put Curse and boyfriend in the same sentence.

"I really do love your cleaning," Dale said, pulling her out of her thoughts.

You're not out of the woods yet. Clean this bastard's house and get gone.

"Good. I'm glad my services please you." She tucked the bottom sheet underneath the mattress.

"I don't suppose you'll look under the bed. I'm sure the wife dropped something under there this morning."

His wife was always conveniently missing whenever she came around to work.

Last time, Mia. Last time of working for this creep.

Kneeling down, she looked under the bed to find something glinting. Mia reached under to grasp the jewel. "I've got it."

She jerked, slamming her head against the wooden slats of the bed as fingers ran up her leg.

"So soft. I knew you'd be soft to the touch."

"Get off me."

Mia tried to climb out, but he stood with one foot between her thighs.

Think, Mia, think.

"You've been teasing me with this body on display." She'd worn her waitressing uniform as she was at the diner immediately after finishing Dale's home.

"Leave me alone. I'm not teasing you. You're seeing stuff that isn't there." She tried to move back, but her butt hit his thigh keeping her in place. Cringing, she tightened her fist around the jewel. She cursed her actions over and over as he proceeded to stroke her thighs.

Would she fit underneath the bed? If her ass was small enough she'd make it out the other side.

He grabbed her ankle, jerked up her dress and tugged. For a slender man, he had a lot of muscle. She cried out as her leg gave out and she fell to the floor. Clawing at the carpet, she tried with all of her might to stay underneath.

"You're not running from me anymore. I want to know what that pretty pussy feels like."

In one yank, she was tugged from underneath the bed. She screamed as the carpet rubbed against her flesh. The uniform she wore provided little protection against the onslaught. She released the jewel and tried to stop him from hurting her.

The moment she was out from under the bed, he turned her over. Slapping out her arms, she hit out. Dale backed away, but she didn't know how long for.

Without wasting a moment, she climbed to her feet and started for the door. Dale's hands grabbed her hair and tugged her back. She collapsed against him, and he threw her into the wooden wardrobe. The door cracked, and for several seconds she was winded from being thrown against the hard surface. Dale picked her up and threw her to the bed. Her dress tore from his rough handling.

Fight.

He charged at the bed, and she kicked him in the stomach. Dale went down, grunting. Scrambling off the bed, she ran for the door trying to get away from him as fast as she could. She screamed in pain as he caught her hair. Thrown against the wall, she wasn't prepared for his slap.

"You little bitch. You're going to learn your place."

His hands went around her neck, cutting off her oxygen. She clawed at his hands. Nothing was helping. Reaching out, she scratched his face, and he released her. The attack went on. Dale slapped her around the face, landing blows to her body. Mia fought, wishing Curse was near to help her. No one was going to save her. Grabbing the lightshade on the drawer beside the bed, she slammed it against Dale so hard. With him following behind her, she wouldn't make it out of the house alive.

Locking herself in the bathroom, she tugged the phone off the wall. The door shook under the impact of his body.

Dialing Ashley's number took her two attempts. Her hands were shaking so hard, she couldn't even focus. Tears fell down her face, and she worked fast.

The phone rang, and she jumped as Dale threw his body against the door.

"Come on, Ashley, pick up."

"Get out here, bitch. I'm going to fuck you and make sure you can't stand for the rest of your life. I'll fuck up that pretty face of yours. No one will come near you." His threats poured out. Fear gripped her with every passing second.

"Who is this?" Ashley asked.

"Ashley, I need your help."

"Mia, what's wrong?"

She heard Curse in the background.

"Dale Worthington attacked me. I'm locked in his bathroom. Please, I can't fight him. He's a lot stronger than I thought. I'm—" She cried out as the door rattled again.

"Mia?"

"I'm scared. Please."

"Shit, Curse—"

"Mia, what's going on?"

His voice filled her with warmth. She sobbed down the line. "Please, come and get me. I'm so scared." She screamed again as the door was slammed once again.

"Listen to me, look through his shit and find something to use to protect yourself with. I don't give a fuck what it is. Find something to hurt him." She got up off the toilet and started to do as Curse asked. "Anything pointy or sharp."

Opening doors she found bottles of pills, razors, bath soaps. Nothing else and she told him as much.

"Use the toilet brush. It's dirty, but it will hurt him enough. It'll give us some time."

Nodding, she grabbed the brush and held it away from her. The thing was dirty, but she kept a firm hold on it.

"Come quickly, Curse, please."

"I'll be there as fast as I can." The phone went dead.

Panic clawed at her as she watched the door. The time went by, and all the time she tried to count numbers off the top of her head.

He'll come. He'll protect you.

"When I get in there, you little slut, no one is going to save you. I'm going to fuck your pussy, take your ass, and squeeze the fucking life out of you."

She whimpered, holding the phone like a lifeline.

Come on, Curse. Save me where no one else can.

Her face was starting to hurt. Touching the side of her face, she winced at the sudden pain. Everything hurt, and glancing down at her uniform she saw it was torn, exposing her bra and some of her stomach.

"Fucking locks," he said growling out the words.

Closing her eyes, she started to count the number of times he threw his body against the door. Her hand shook from holding the toilet brush. It was only a matter of time before he finally got into the room. Rubbing her eyes with her free hand, she tried to think logically as a man was intent on raping and hurting her.

You can do this, Mia.

The last man who scared the life out of her was no longer around. She'd taken care of him and would do it again.

He didn't know you were coming.

She wasn't strong enough to fight off Dale.

The only person she could count on was Curse.

Chapter Eight

Ashley had many uses in life, and the main one was knowing shit loads about the town she grew up in. She took the lead on the back of Pussy's bike. Curse followed behind her, losing his shit inside his head at the threat Mia was under. How he kept his cool at her pleading he didn't know. She sounded so lost, so broken. If she was harmed, he was going to cause so many fucking problems, the guy was going to wish he'd not hired her as a cleaner.

She's got to be fine.

Mia's a fighter. He liked that about her, but even an expert fighter in life lost a fight or two.

They stopped at a large house not far from where Jerry lived. Climbing off his bike, he went straight for the front door. He heard Pussy and Ashley following behind him. Not waiting for someone to answer his knock, he grabbed a rock from the garden and smashed it through the window. The door looked like the kind that would hurt if he tried to slam through it. Rich folk were always worried about being robbed and tended to spend extra money on security. He flicked the lock into place, and the moment he entered the house, he heard the screams.

His woman's feminine cries and a male's more masculine words were heard easily in the house.

Going for the stairs, Curse only had one person in mind, Mia. He needed to get her out of here and to safety.

"Leave me alone." Her scream tore at his soul.

Heart pounding he charged up the stairs. Half way up the steps he heard the unmistakable sound of wood splintering apart.

Mia's screams got louder. She shouted and

begged for someone to leave her alone.

Running the last of the way he charged into the main bedroom then ran into the bathroom. She was fighting, crying as a slender man was tearing at her underwear trying to get them off.

Acting without thinking, Curse tugged the fucker off her, wrapping both of his arms around the guy's waist and throwing him against the wall.

Ashley and Pussy crashed into the room seconds later.

"Get her out of here, now. Jerry lives close by. Take her to him. I'll sort this fucker out."

He waited for them to leave the room.

Dale got to his feet, wiping some blood off his lip. "Are you her keeper?"

Not answering, Curse fisted his hands ready to kill this bastard.

"You're not answering. I have to say I'm not surprised. She's such a nice piece of ass. I didn't believe for a moment that she was alone." Dale climbed to his feet.

"Your first biggest mistake was thinking you could touch her at all. She's mine." Curse faced the other man, waiting for the other man to pounce. The anger inside him was growing. He wanted to kill this man, hurt him for hurting his woman. Before Mia was taken out of his sight he'd already seen the damage done. He'd not seen everything, but he'd seen enough to know this man was living on borrowed fucking time.

"That supposed to scare me?" Dale asked, facing off. "You don't think I can take you?"

"I'd like to see you try and take me."

Come on, fucker, lash out. Make the first move.

"She cleans for me, man. Bitch was asking for it."

Those words were the final straw. Charging at

him, Curse landed a blow to Dale's face, sending him crashing to the floor.

"You wanted to mess with a woman because she could do fuck all about it. Let's see how you fight a real fucking man."

Curse landed blow after blow, aiming for the face, ribs, stomach, and everything to hurt him. Grabbing the bastard's head, he pushed him face first through the shower stall. The glass smashed, but Curse kept on going. The blood was dripping from Dale's face.

When he was bored of trying to hurt him, he landed punch after punch against the man's face. In his mind he saw Mia's uniform hanging off her shoulder. The bruises were already appearing on her face from this bastard's attack when he sent her away.

"Curse," Pussy said, shouting his name.

He couldn't stop. Blow after blow, he fucked up the man's face.

"You're going to have to make him stop." Jerry's voice penetrated his mind. "The bastard is dead."

"Curse, stop now!" The final voice belonged to Devil. Curse's fist was raised ready to land another punch.

Turning to his left he saw Devil, Jerry, Pussy, and a couple of his brothers standing, watching him.

Glancing down before him, he felt nothing about the mess he'd created from his attack. Dale was unrecognizable. Blood soaked the cream blankets, and he climbed off, aware of the wetness coating his clothes. His hands were bruised, covered with a layer of blood.

"He attacked a woman," Curse said, staring at his crew. They were not looking at him with disgust. Each person was figuring out what they had to do to help him.

"It doesn't matter, Curse. This guy was going to be dead in a matter of days," Jerry said. "There's a target out for his head. The wife and kid were long gone. They've been gone for a long time."

"A target on his head?"

"Yeah, he raped a friend of mine's girl. When I say friend, I mean proper mafia, don't fuck off and do as you're told kind of friend. I was supposed to keep him alive until Frederick was due to arrive next week. This fucker was working for Frederick when he attacked one of his men's women." Jerry stared at the mess and pulled out his cell phone. "This is why I only ever offer small fucking favors. Frederick doesn't give a fuck about anyone, but taking vengeance was an act of business, not sympathy."

The other man disappeared, and Curse heard him talking in hushed tones.

"I'm sorry, Devil,"

"No, you're not. If this fucker was attacking Lexie, I'd have done the same." Devil whistled as he looked at the body. "This reminds me why we rarely stay in the same fucking place. This kind of shit is a nightmare."

"We burn the body? House fire, bad mains and all that shit?" Ripper asked, stepping around Death.

"No, the cops have already reported there are too many suspicious fires just lately," Jerry said. "Fredrick has a guy arriving tomorrow. One of us has to stay with the body, and his guy will do whatever's necessary to make this fucker disappear without a problem."

"A mass clean up?" Devil asked.

"We get to see the professionals do the job." Jerry agreed, staring at the body then at Curse. "You're going to have to stay behind. This guy is a professional, and he'll get everything off you. I suggest you take a shower and try to keep the shit contained to this room. I'll also need to talk with you, Devil. Frederick's pissed, and he wants to know what you're prepared to do about it."

"I don't give a fuck what he wants," Devil said.

"This is not the kind of man you fuck with." Jerry didn't look happy. In fact, the pimp looked positively scared shitless.

Curse shook his head. "What about Mia? She's covered in evidence."

"She stays at my place. Melanie is still gone, and she's not coming back any time soon. I'll keep an eye on her, and I promise I won't fuck with her or suggest she become a call girl," Jerry said.

"I'm going to need to talk to her," Curse said.

Staying away from her after this was going to be a fucking nightmare.

"You've got to think about this, Curse," Devil said, speaking up.

"What do you mean?" He turned to look at his president. The respect he had for Devil would never disappear, but he also knew that Devil would do whatever needed to be done.

"If she's your old lady we don't have a problem." He waited for Devil to finish. "If she's not then we've got a problem, Curse. She has to go, and I don't mean on a long vacation. I mean she has to go six feet under the fucking ground."

"No," he said, shaking his head. "She doesn't need to do that shit."

"Your call to make," Devil said.

He stood staring at the mess on the bed and wondered what the fuck had happened in the last couple of hours. Hearing Mia's pleas for help had awoken the protector inside him. Curse didn't regret what he'd done. She wasn't the problem. This mess he'd created was the problem.

"She's my old lady. You leave her alone, and I'll

deal with her."

"Are you sure about this, man?" Pussy asked. "An old lady is some serious shit."

"I'm sure. She's my old lady."

Devil stood for several minutes and watched him before nodding. "Fine, she's an old lady. I'll make Lexie aware of it, and she'll talk to Phoebe. They'll be no keeping her away from everyone."

"I know. Just give me time. Let me deal with this." He pointed at the blood and the mess. "Then I'll handle Mia."

She would have no choice but to do as she was told.

"Okay. Death, you stay with him, and Pussy, get back to Ashley. Inform her of what is going on. Tell her to keep her crap to herself."

Pussy agreed and left. One by one the men left, and Death sat outside the door where there was no blood.

"This fucking sucks," Death said. "I was going to spend the next week fucking. Now, I've got to babysit your ass."

"You were going to fuck not find an excuse to kill something?" Curse walked into the bathroom. He'd need to clean out the glass first or he could just stand under the shower jet.

"You're not doing a bad job of killing people. I doubt that fucker always looked like that." Death nodded at the dead body.

"Whatever. I can't be done with this shit. I fucked up."

"Yeah, you did fuck up. We're putting a stamp on this town, and you've got a dead guy who's wanted by a man we want fuck all to do with."

Glaring at Death, Curse didn't see the use in arguing with him and told him so. "What's done is done.

I can't change anything or bring him back."

"Is she worth it?" Death asked, shouting out the question. With his hand on the doorframe, Curse stopped to think about the question. Was Mia worth all this shit? When she smiled and let go for a few seconds, his heart literally stopped. She was so beautiful and had suffered in life.

"Yes, she's worth it and a hell of a lot more." He entered the bathroom and started to take a shower.

****

Mia cried as Ashley ran a bath in Jerry's house. She'd not been here since he'd offered her a chance of becoming a call girl. Wiping her nose, she winced at the pain. Every inch of her body ached or hurt from what had happened.

"It's okay, honey. I'll take care of everything."

"It hurts. It all hurts, and it won't stop."

"I know. I'm here, and we're going to help you. Jerry told me you're to take your time. I've already called to the diner and put a call through to your mom." Ashley kept talking, but Mia's head was hurting. Standing up, she wobbled over to the mirror and winced. She was a mess. Dale had landed several blows to her face. She had bruising down the right side of her face, a bleeding lip, and it also looked like there was a cut across her eyebrow.

Purple bruises rose up around her neck. They stood out against her pale skin where he'd choked her.

You're safe now. He's not coming back.

Curse had come to her rescue, saving her.

Ashley appeared behind her. "Mia, stop looking at yourself. It's not going to do any good, and you're only going to get upset."

"I hurt."

"I know, honey."

She followed Ashley to the bath and removed the remains of her clothing. Her uniform was a mess from Dale's rough handling.

"He was an animal, Mia."

"I don't want to talk about it." She stepped out of the uniform and the bra. Her panties were torn from her body, and they were back at the house.

Closing her eyes, she lowered herself into the warm water, wincing as it sloshed over her cuts.

"I'm here. I'm going to get rid of this. Please, stay here."

The door to the bathroom opened. She wrapped her arms around her legs, drawing them against her chest.

"You can't go in there," Ashley said.

"I'm going to pass on a message. Don't tell me what to do," Pussy said.

She heard some shuffling outside the door. Pressing her head to her knees, she heard Ashley sigh.

"She's hurting right now."

"Those clothes need to go back to the house. Give them to Death. He'll know what to do." Pussy spoke the final order. Seconds later she heard the front door opening and closing.

Looking up, she saw Pussy standing in the doorway.

He didn't avert his gaze as she stared back at him.

"Where's Curse?" she asked, wishing he was there to hold her. The only man she trusted near her was Curse.

"Something has come up. He's having to stay at the house for the next twenty-four hours until someone comes to clean up the mess." Pussy sat down on the toilet. He stared down at his closed palms.

"Dale's dead, isn't he?"

"You're not surprised by that?"

She shook her head. "He was going to hurt me, really hurt me."

"Babe, I hate to break this to you, but you're not exactly looking all with it right now. The fucker did hurt you."

Mia winced at the memory of Dale's hands on her. "I was an idiot. I let my guard down once, and he was there ready to pounce."

Tears fell from her eyes. She felt them run down her cheeks dropping into the water.

"What were you thinking?" Pussy asked.

She stared at him. He wasn't looking at her body but at her face. There was nothing sexual in his look. Pussy looked freaked out about something.

"What's going on?"

"Curse has encountered some problems. The club is handling it, but I want you to answer some of my questions to see if you're worthy of our trust." Mia wanted to argue but chose to remain silent. After everything she'd been through, she wasn't in the mood to fight with anyone, least of all Curse's friend. "If you knew how dangerous Dale was, why did you continue to work for him?"

"I needed the money."

"Curse would have given it to you."

"Stop!" She sobbed the word out, glaring at him. "I'm sleeping with Curse. To the outside world we're boyfriend and girlfriend. I'm not going to be like the club whores who take from him for sex. I will not be the same. I can earn my keep and take care of me and my mom. I don't need anyone to take care of me." She wiped at her eyes and tried her hardest to keep her emotions together. "I want to be different when it comes to Curse. So many other women have taken from him. I want to be the one who he doesn't have to pay."

During the time they'd been together Curse had invaded her heart, and now she was trapped with her feelings. She'd fallen for him, and Mia wanted to mean more to him than a quick fuck.

He saved me.

Blowing out a breath, she turned her gaze back to Pussy.

"You're in love with him."

She didn't dispute his words.

"Does he even know how you feel?"

"No, he doesn't know, and he doesn't need to know yet. This is a bit of fun to him. I was a challenge because I didn't fall at his feet." Pussy was a good looking man. He had long hair tied at the back. His body was thick, tight, coiled muscles. She saw why Ashley liked him. "When this is all over he's going to want to leave. I'm not going to be everything he needs. He'll realize the truth very soon."

"You're wrong. You've got no idea what he's done to protect you and the club."

The sound of the front door opening filled the room.

"Ashley's back. I'm going to leave you to your wash. Get cleaned up and spend the rest of the day relaxing. I'll drop by to see your mother."

He was at the door when she told him to stop.

"I needed the money for my mom. Her medical bills have never stopped. She needs to be taken care of, and that's what I do and what I pay for. I don't spend the money elsewhere. It all goes on my mom." She chanced a look at him.

His expression was closed off.

"I'll take care of everything." Pussy nodded at her and left the bathroom. Keeping hold of her legs, she heard Ashley enter. Her friend looked pale, and as she reached for the soap her hands were shaking.

"Hey, honey. You're going to end up all wrinkly if you stay in the water too long." Ashley kept talking.

"What's going on?" Mia asked.

"Nothing is going on. Just be glad you're here and not at Dale's. I promise you, everything will be fine. Jerry is in his office dealing with some stuff. I've just been with him and Devil talking a few things through. You don't need to worry about a thing. I'm taking care of you. We're going to have a girly day here. I think some movies, ice-cream." Her words went on and on about what they could do with the remainder of the day.

Mia ignored her suggestions, knowing in her heart something bad had happened. Closing her eyes, she let Ashley wash her body, and when it was time to get out, she wrapped her body in a towel.

"I'm going to let you get dressed. I'll grab a first aid kit."

A knock sounded, and Mia called for whoever it was to enter, hoping it was Curse.

Disappointment swamped her as Jerry stood on the other side. "I brought this for you." He held a red first aid box.

"Thank you, I was going to go and get one." Ashley took the box and handed it to her.

Mia took it keeping her eyes on Jerry.

"Ashley, will you go and get me a drink? I could really use a chocolate or coffee." She smiled at her friend, trying to get rid of her.

"Don't you need me with you?" Ashley asked.

"No, I can mend up my cuts and bruises."

She waited for the other woman to leave before focusing on Jerry. "Tell me what's going on, please? Pussy has been by, and I've seen how Ashley looks. What's going on?"

"What makes you think I'm going to let you know the details of everything happening?" Jerry asked, entering the bathroom.

Her body was covered by a large white robe.

"You respect me and know I can handle whatever is going on." She faced him without flinching.

He rested his hands on his hips, staring at her.

"Curse killed the man who attacked you. Dale Worthington has been wanted by a man I know. He's not a very nice man, and Curse has taken the satisfaction out of killing him. He's also fucked up a very important business deal for this man. Dale was the icing on top of the cake, so to speak. His death was supposed to be the gift that Frederick gave to this man. Dale is dead now, and my boss can't offer his friend the gift. Do you get my meaning?" She got it. Dale was supposed to die, but only in the way that the other person chose. She listened to Jerry, knowing this wasn't going to be the last she heard of it.

"So, Curse is in danger."

"We're waiting for one of his men to come and clean up the mess. It will be up to Frederick what he does with Curse and the Chaos Bleeds crew afterward."

"They're not nice people," she asked, feeling childish.

"No, they're not nice people, and Curse will do well to keep his head down for the time being."

She stared at the box in her hands. "Will they hurt him?"

"Devil won't let them hurt him. Chaos Bleeds are a crew, and they stick by each other. Whatever Frederick wants, he'll get within reason. Just try to keep Curse out of danger. That man will do anything to protect you, and he's more than happy to kill for you."

"We're only dating," she said.

"Then you're a fool. That man is in love with you. Open your eyes before you do something you'll regret and do get him killed."

Jerry left her alone. Staring at the closed door, her heart was pounding after his words. Curse loved her? Surely not, there was no way he could love her. They hadn't been together all that long.

You're in love with him.

Closing her eyes, she tried to stop herself from feeling the pain that the knowledge filled her with.

Chapter Nine

Curse stood in the room as the man came in. He was wearing a business suit as he looked at the body. Alfred, his name was, and the man didn't give either him or Death the time of day. He looked over the body, pulled his cell phone out and made a call.

"Hey, boss, yeah, this fucker is dead. No, it wasn't an easy death. Dale died slow and painfully." Alfred looked at them. "Are you sure? Okay I'll handle it."

The cell phone was pocketed, and Curse faced the man, waiting to see what the outcome was.

"My boss is not happy. Frederick likes to get his own way, and he had a certain torture planned for this man. However, I see you hurt him, and my boss is prepared to let this infraction slide for now."

"That's good," Death said, looking happy.

"He wants to meet with Devil and the rest of Chaos Bleeds."

There was a noise at the door, and Curse turned to see three people enter wearing all over white protective equipment. Alfred gave them instructions in a foreign language, one that Curse didn't recognize.

"We need you to strip down. We'll wash you, remove all evidence, and there are clothes waiting for you out in the hallway," Alfred said.

"What does your boss want with us?" Curse asked, removing his clothes. He'd never been shy about his body, and getting naked in front of a bunch of strangers didn't bother him.

"Consider it business, son. Do as you're told, and everything will go fine." Alfred spoke to the people. The moment he was naked, Curse closed his eyes as he was washed of all evidence of this.

When he was finished, he was shoved out of the door. Death stood there, holding his clothes.

"I suggest we get dressed and get the fuck out of here," Death said. "You can go and see Mia, but Devil wants you back at the clubhouse for a meeting. Shit is going to hit the fan with what happened."

Putting the clothes on, he heard a saw going to work along with the sound of crunching bone.

"Fuck me, let's get out of here." Together they made it out of the front door. His bike was parked up, and he straddled the machine. He didn't ride for long before he parked the bike back up outside of Jerry's place. There was no car in the driveway, and he looked back at Death.

"He's at the clubhouse. It's a business meeting for all of us."

Nodding, Curse entered the front door. Ashley appeared first, poking her head around the door frame.

"Hey," she said.

"Where is she?" Curse asked.

"I'm here." Mia stepped around her friend. Seeing her filled him with relief.

Opening up his arms, she stepped inside them. He held onto her tightly. The bruises on her face and neck made him angry, but the man was dead. Curse knew he couldn't kill the same man twice.

"I was so worried," she said.

"I've got you."

"I can't believe you came for me." She sobbed the words against his neck. "I didn't expect you to come for me. I thought I was going to die yesterday."

Jerking back, he stroked her cheek. "Baby, I'd never leave you like that."

She wrapped her arms around him, holding on.

Closing his eyes, he did something he'd never

done, he sent up a prayer to whoever was willing to listen to him. He didn't know what he would have done if he'd not gotten there in time. The very thought left him feeling sick and hollow inside.

"We'll talk more when I get back. I just needed to see you before I went to the clubhouse."

Ashley gave them privacy walking back into the sitting room. Curse watched her leave before turning back to Mia.

"I'm fine. She's keeping me company. I don't want to go home. Too many questions and my mom knows when I'm lying."

"When I get back from this meeting, we've got to talk. There's stuff you need to know."

She nodded. "I guessed as much."

"Stay here. Don't answer the door to anyone, and whoever keeps ringing the door, call us and we'll be here as quickly as possible," he said.

"I will."

He dropped a kiss to her lips. "Take care."

Leaving the house, he made sure the door was locked before heading back to his bike.

"Fuck me, you are in love," Death said.

"Shut your fucking mouth. You don't know shit." Straddling his bike, Curse turned the key and headed toward the clubhouse. Death was right behind him. He kept a steady pace and climbed off the bike. Several of the women were standing outside of the building, smoking. He stared at them in their short skirts or shorts. None of them held any appeal to him, and it made him laugh at how much he'd loved fucking them.

"They're all for me now," Death said. "Everyone is falling in love. I tell you, The Skulls are fucking cursed. I'm staying well away from them whenever they're in town."

Laughing, Curse entered the clubhouse to find all of the club members waiting for them. They were not in the privacy of the office. Devil was talking to all of them, and Jerry was there also.

"Frederick has called. He's going to be here by Friday," Devil said. "He wants to see all of us, including you and Mia."

"What does he want with Mia?" Curse asked.

"He wants to see the woman responsible for killing Dale and losing him a shitload of money. Frederick has a deal in place with a transport firm. They transport the coke, girls, and guns that Frederick sells as part of his business. Only, Dale had raped this man's girl, and seeing as Frederick owned him, it was a gift from one business man to another. Now, Dale is dead, and Frederick doesn't have anyone to do his transport for him. Curse fucked up a deal as Frederick's not going to make any money as he can't get the product from one state to another." Devil glared at him.

"Do we have any reason to believe that he poses a threat to all of us?" Ripper asked. "After everything that's happened to Judi, I don't want her hurt anymore."

"No, she won't be hurt. This is between the club and Frederick."

"Then why does he want to meet Mia?" Curse asked, forcing the words out through gritted teeth.

"Judi's not the one responsible for killing a wanted man," Devil snapped, shouting out the words.

"Frederick is not the kind of man to cross. He's the shark in a pond full of fish. In comparison, we're all the fish," Jerry said.

"Did you have any idea she was cleaning for that prick?" Curse asked. He was looking for anyone to blame other than himself. She shouldn't have been alone in a strange man's home.

"No, I didn't have the first fucking clue. In case you didn't notice I run a business and have a wife of my own." Jerry folded his arms over his chest.

"Yeah, you're so fucking busy that you suggest my woman become a call girl and happen to be a fucking lapdog for a man you consider a fucking danger to all of us." Curse shouted, letting all of his aggression out into the words.

"I can do what the fuck I like, and if I want to work for Frederick, then I'll work for him. I've been working for and with him the last fifteen years. You want to fuck with me then go ahead, Curse. You and the club will not last ten minutes alone with him. I'm doing you all a favor letting you know what you're in for." Jerry shook his head. "Fuck this. I got a wife to keep happy and shit to deal with. I'll see you all on Friday. I advise you don't start organizing a party anytime soon."

Jerry left the clubhouse. The echo of the door slamming closed behind him filled the main room.

"Keep your shit together, Curse. I don't know who the fuck this man is, but whoever he is has Jerry scared. We keep to ourselves, and you better stay the fuck out of trouble until Friday. I don't give a fuck what you have to do, but stay out of the way." Devil stood, looking around the clubhouse. "Clean this shit up. We settled down to live a good life. None of you are giving us a chance to have such a life."

"What about The Skulls?" Death asked. "Should we call them?"

"No, we shouldn't. They've got their own set of problems. We can handle this shit. I'm going home to my wife. Stay out of the fucking way of trouble."

Curse watched his president leave. Regretting his words, he followed Devil outside.

"I'm sorry," Curse said.

Devil turned to look at him. "The moment we agreed to settle down in Piston County, we all agreed to keep our heads locked firmly on. We're vulnerable when we stay in one place, but we're also stronger than ever before."

"I know."

"Shut your fucking mouth. I got no problem with you killing that man. He was hurting your woman, would have raped her if given the chance." Devil ran a hand down his face. "No, what I hate is knowing what's going to happen if this fucker chooses, and you know what that could mean."

Curse knew that they could end up as Frederick's lap dogs if he chose.

"I know."

"Good. Go to your woman, Curse. Let her know what's going to happen and then be here Friday. If everything goes well, we'll be lucky and can call it a day." Devil waved his hand in the air as if pushing their troubles aside.

Curse watched as he climbed on the back of his bike and headed out of the compound.

"Devil's worried," Pussy said from behind him.

Turning toward his friend, Curse nodded. "Yeah, I know, and it's all my fault."

"No, it's not. Mia needed you, and you lost it. There's nothing we can do about it." Pussy slapped him on the back. "You were right. Mia is something special. She's got a lot of love inside her and a lot of pain as well."

Nodding, he moved toward his bike. "I'll be back on Friday. Take care of everything for me."

"Okay."

He headed toward Jerry's house. The other man's car was parked, and he parked his bike up, walking up the steps to knock on the door.

Mia answered his knock. She looked relieved to see him. "Thank God. I was so worried that I wouldn't see you again."

"Where's Ashley?" Curse asked.

"I'm here." The other woman stood behind Mia.

"Do you want a ride to the clubhouse?" Curse looked at the other woman, wondering what was going on in her mind. She looked scared of him. He didn't blame her. She'd seen the damage he'd done to Dale.

"No, I'm going to stay here with Jerry. He'll give me a lift back to the clubhouse when it's needed."

Handing Mia a helmet, Curse climbed on his bike and waited for her. He watched as she hugged her friend then got on the back of his bike.

"Thank you for waiting for me," she said, whispering against his ear.

Not responding, he pulled out of the house and headed for the open road. No one was staying at the house out on the beaten track. Curse wanted to have a few hours to call his own before their problems caught up to them.

****

When Jerry entered the house and started drinking, Ashley had looked concerned. Leaving Ashley behind, Mia hoped to feel secure, but the way Curse was acting left her feeling scared. Mia stared at Curse and knew something bad was about to happen to all of them. Dale Worthington had started all this. His touch had repulsed her, and yet they were all about to be a in a lot of trouble for Dale's death.

"He was a wanted man. Some guy called Frederick was waiting for the right opportunity to come and claim him. Mafia shit or something like one of those movies," Curse said.

"I used to watch gangster movies. Is everything they say on them true?" She took a seat, lowering herself into the chair.

"Yes, and it can be worse." He ran fingers through his hair. She caught sight of the cuts on his knuckles. "On Friday we're to go and meet him at the clubhouse. He's going to want to know why we killed him and what we got out of it."

"Okay." What more could she say? This sounded serious, even dangerous to her.

"There's more."

He turned away from her to look outside the window. She gazed at the length of his back. The tension inside him caught at her heart. Mia had caused this because of her stupid fucking pride. If only she'd accepted the money from him, she wouldn't have continued working for Dale and causing problems.

"To the club, you're now my old lady."

"What does that mean?" She'd heard Ashley refer to some of the women as old ladies. The respect in Ashley's voice was hard to ignore when she heard about them.

"It means you're my woman, and when we get the time, we're going to get married."

As far as proposals went, this one sucked.

She locked her fingers together and stared at him, waiting for whatever else he had to say.

"If I didn't agree to have you as my woman then you'd be taken care of. The club would have to get rid of you as you were a liability."

"And we can't have me being a liability, right?" she asked, tears filling her eyes.

Mia didn't know why she was hurt by being ordered to get married. It wasn't like there was a man waiting to wine and dine her. No, the only prospect she had was Curse.

You're in love with him.

The pain hurt too much thinking of him being forced into marrying her when he really didn't want to.

Biting her lip, she gazed down at the table feeling sorry for herself.

"Mia, I didn't have a choice." He took hold of her hand, kneeling in front of her.

"It's not that."

"Then why are you crying?"

"I don't know. Nothing makes sense to me anymore."

He kissed her knuckles. Curse stroked her cheek and she winced at the pain.

"Shit, I'm sorry. I would take the pain away from you if I could."

"We all know you can't play God, Curse. This pain is what I deserve." Looking away from the sincerity in his face, she stared down at her hands. "You once asked what happened with Ashley."

"Mia, you don't have to do this," he said.

"Yes, if we're going to get married then I'm not going to let you do this without knowing the truth. I'm not some weak-willed girl you have to take care of, Curse."

Pushing hair out of her face, she turned in her seat to look at him in the face. "Ashley's mother died when she was born. It was only her and her father for the longest time. He was a nice man for the most part. I liked him. He was more than happy to have me around for her." The memories were bitter, the truth harder for her to realize.

"Anyway, Ashley was a cheerleader in high school while I was a book nerd. I was always into the books, and I didn't want to do anything else. I was more than happy to be confined to the library rather than go out and do other things."

For so long she'd kept this story to herself.

"She changed. Not overnight but it took months. She became withdrawn, and she started wanting boys to notice her. I remember the clothes getting shorter, and she'd snap at her father. Ashley stopped letting me sleep over at her home, and she always came to my place."

A lump filled in her throat.

"Shit, Mia."

"No, you're going to listen. You wanted to know the truth. This is me giving you the complete truth. I've never told anyone else this. On prom night Ashley was late. I was meeting her at the school, and we were going together." Licking her lips, she tightened her grip in his hands. "I took a cab to her home. The lights were on in her bedroom. I opened the door like I had all the time growing up. The moment I entered the house I heard Ashley begging and pleading for him to stop."

The memories crashed over her, but she forced them out.

"I went upstairs. Her prom dress was torn. The dress she took hours picking. I hated seeing that torn dress, but then I saw what was happening. Her father was raping her. I couldn't believe it. I don't know how long I stood there, but it couldn't have been long. He might have stopped, I don't know."

Tears filled her eyes and spilled over.

"Baby, stop."

She shook her head. "No, I'm not going to stop. He told her to be a good little girl like she'd always been." Wiping at her nose, she gasped around the pain squeezing her chest. "I heard the fight go out of her. My best friend in the whole world had been attacked by her father years ago and I didn't even know. In the corner I spotted the metal lightshade. She loved the lightshade. I think it was her mother's before it was hers. Without thinking, I grabbed it and smashed it over his head. I didn't stop. He was inside her, and I just kept hitting him. The blood was everywhere, but I didn't care. Ashley screamed for me to stop. She shoved him away from her, and I kept hitting him. I didn't stop. I couldn't stop. She ended up grabbing my arms to stop me from hurting him."

"This is why he went missing a couple of days after prom night, but you told the cops he went out that night and never returned?"

"I failed her. I killed him. We checked for a pulse, but he was dead."

Licking her lips, the tears fell down her cheeks, and she wiped them away gently.

"What did you do?" he asked.

"We wrapped his body in a shower curtain. I could drive; Ashley couldn't. We stored him in my car and drove him out to middle of nowhere. We buried him deep into the earth. I was going to go to the police, but she wouldn't let me. She told me not to go down for him. When we got back, we scrubbed the house clean. In the backyard we burned our dresses and everything we wore."

Curse pulled up a chair, and he cupped her cheeks.

"Baby, look at me," he said.

She returned her gaze to his.

"You waited the weekend and said he went out that night."

Mia nodded. "Yes. We stayed home. No one saw me at the school. We stayed in eating ice-cream and cursing all men. No one has ever found him, and Ashley didn't return to his house. Ashley took the money her mother left her, and she stayed with me for some time before I went away to college. I kept this secret for a long time. I've got blood on my hands, Curse. I'm not some innocent woman."

He pressed his lips to hers, and she moaned. She didn't expect him to kiss her like this after what she told him.

"Why?" she asked, breaking away from his lips.

"Do you really think I'm innocent?" He ran his thumb along her lip. "I've killed more than one sick fuck who needed it, Mia. You shouldn't stop yourself from loving or being with a man because of guilt. That fucker doesn't deserve you to think about him. He was raping his own daughter. Don't give him the satisfaction of letting him win."

"I'm dirty, Curse."

"No." He forced her to look at him. "You're not dirty. You're beautiful." He pressed his lips to hers. "You're my woman, Mia. You'll listen to me, or I will put you over my knee, understood?"

"Yes, I understand."

Wrapping her arms around him, she held on tightly to Curse. He was her lifeline, the chance to have something more than the pain that she had always felt.

Chapter Ten

Curse held her as she sobbed against his chest. Her breath fanned across his neck, and through it all he held her. His cock tightened at the feel of her against him. Mia's body was soft to his hard. Her breasts pushed against his chest distracting him.

Come on, fucker, stay down. She's hurting.

His cock didn't care. Mia was close, and he wanted to fuck her.

From the moment Whizz told him about Ashley's father who disappeared he figured the two women had something to do with it. He didn't care that Mia had killed the man. From the sound of it, the fucker needed to die for screwing his daughter. Thinking about Ashley, he now knew why she always looked in pain. Sleeping with every man she met helped her not to make any commitment. The club didn't ask for a detailed description of their sexual past. Providing there was no sexual disease no one cared about what happened in people's past.

Picking Mia up in his arms, he carried her upstairs.

"Where are we going?" she asked.

"I'm taking you upstairs to bed. I want to hold you, make love to you, and force the rest of the world to disappear. The only way I get to do that is to be with you like this."

She wrapped her body around him, and he lowered her to her feet at the bottom of the bed.

"Curse?"

He pressed a finger to her lips. "No. I don't care what you did. No one is perfect, and I never expected you to be perfect. When I saw you in the diner, Mia, I wanted you. I wanted to fuck you and call you my woman. I've got to do that, and nothing you say is going to change that."

Fingering the end of her shirt, he worked it up her body. She wore a plain grey sports bra.

"Jerry loaned me the clothes. His wife won't be too happy with her clothes being used," Mia said, folding her arms across her breasts.

Taking hold of her hands, he pushed them out of his way. "You don't get to hide from me. I like seeing your body on display, and it'll never change for me." Reaching around her, he unsnapped the bra and started to drag the straps from her body. He was careful not to touch any of bruises or her cuts.

"I love you, Curse."

He paused. Tilting her head back, he stared into her eyes.

"I know you don't feel the same way, but I wanted you to know that I've fallen in love with you." She laughed. "Great, I've gone and said it twice."

Claiming her lips, he stopped her from talking. She loved him, and happiness filled him at knowing the truth. Stroking her cheek, he smiled into her eyes.

"I love you, too."

"You don't have to say anything." She stared down at the floor.

Curse tilted her head back. "It's something I can't control. I love you, and I don't give a fuck about the trouble I've caused, baby. Dale touched you." He lightly touched her cheek where the bruises were stood out in stark contrast to her pale skin. "I will kill every person who tries to hurt you, who even threatens to hurt you. I love you."

She wrapped her arms around his neck.

Running his hands down her back, he gripped her ass and rubbed his cock against her. "Feel how much I need you."

Her moan vibrated through her body. Curse fingered the sweatpants she wore. Shoving them down her body, he watched them pool at her feet. She didn't wear any panties.

Mia worked his pants off. He removed his jacket throwing it over to the other side of the room. Kicking the jeans aside, he sank his fingers into her hair, fisting the length. She made no motion of pain, and he pulled her head back to expose her lips to his kiss. Plunging his tongue into her mouth, he tasted her. She moaned, opening her lips for him to explore.

"I've got you, baby," Curse said. "I've got you for the rest of our lives, and I'm never letting you go, not for anyone."

He laid gentle kisses to her bruises, making sure not to hurt her. The purple marks around her neck made him angry at the ease with which he'd killed the other man. Her voice was a little hoarse when she spoke but not enough to change how she sounded.

Sitting on the end of the bed, he tugged her between his thighs. No words were necessary as he skimmed his fingers up the outside of her thighs. Her body shook as he stroked her, taking his time over her flesh. He hated seeing the evidence of the pain she'd been in. Each bruise was a testament to his failure to protect her. Curse should have forced her to take the money.

They'd done things her way. It was time for her to realize her way sucked. In the future they were going to do it his way.

"Open your legs."

She didn't argue with him and proceeded to open her thighs for him. He stared at her creamy slit covered in a fine dusting of pubic hair.

"This is mine," he said, reaching out to slide a finger through her wet heat. "No other man is going to know what you feel like when you come. Only my dick, fingers, and mouth are going to know how fucking ripe you are for dick."

"Stop it, Curse. Other men don't matter to me."

"Good. Because you love me, things are about to get a whole lot dirtier." Curse needed to give her everything inside him without letting anything back. Stroking through her slit, he pressed his thumb to her nub. "Are you too sore to take what I can give you?"

"No, I'm not too sore. I want you, Curse. I need you." The words fell from her lips on a gasp as he slid two fingers straight into her core. He didn't give her a chance to grow accustomed to the sudden intrusion, and he added in another finger. Curse stretched her cunt with three fingers. Her cream soaked the digits and leaked onto his palm.

"You're so fucking desperate for a cock," he said.

"Yes."

Removing his hand, he sucked each finger into his mouth, swallowing down her musky juice as he did.

"Turn around. Bend over."

Mia did as he asked. Her actions were slow, but he was a very patient man. She bent down, cupping her ankles. Curse stared at the perfection before him. The opening of her sex was visible, and she was soaking wet. He stared at her asshole. The puckered entrance of her forbidden hole called to him to take it.

"I'm going to fuck your ass soon, Mia, and you're going to give it to me, aren't you, babe?"

"Yes."

"I'm going to have you screaming in pleasure." Sliding two fingers into her cream, he moved it up to the puckered hole of her ass. She tensed up, and he spanked her. "Don't fucking think of keeping me out, Mia. You're mine."

She relaxed, and he caressed a finger over her ass. The scent of her pussy permeated the air. Leaning forward, he slid his tongue into her cunt as he eased the tip of his finger into her ass.

He pressed on her ass, and she opened up, taking his finger inside her anus. Looking up, he watched his fingers disappear into as he tongued her creamy opening.

"Fuck, Curse."

"I know, but you'll take what I've got to give you." Curse added the second finger into her ass watching her open up underneath him. He stopped as suddenly as he started. "Turn around."

She once again didn't argue with him.

"Get on your knees."

Watching her sink to the floor between his thighs, he gripped his cock.

"Suck."

Her mouth opened, and he fed his length to her lips. Growling, he watched her lips close around his shaft, sucking him inside. Her tongue played over the little slit where his pre-cum came out.

Curse fingered her hair, wrapping the strands around his fist. Gripping her hair, he increased her thrusts on his cock. He went to the back of her throat and pulled away. She licked along the length then pulled off to circle the tip, swallowing down his cream.

"Fuck, you look so fucking beautiful taking my cock into your mouth. You know what you're doing, don't you, baby?"

She murmured her response.

Tugging on her hair, he pulled her lips off his. Helping her to her feet, he slammed his lips down on hers not caring if she didn't like the taste of her own pussy in her mouth. Turning her around, he moved her back until she hit the bed and fell down.

He sank to his knees, caught her legs and spread them open wide. Staring at her pussy, he saw the perfection of her body open and vulnerable for him. Gliding his fingers up her body, he watched her shake beneath his touch.

"I've got you, baby."

She gasped.

Curse opened the lips of her pussy to reveal the jewel of her clit.

"That's what I want." Licking a path from her cunt to her clit, he flicked his tongue over her. She came apart underneath his hands in a matter of seconds, screaming her release. The noise echoed off the walls, but he didn't care. He loved the feel of her coming apart in his arms. Licking her pussy, he swallowed down her cream then plundered her cunt with his tongue.

Her fingers sank into his hair and tugged on the strands.

"Curse?" She cried out his name as he tongued her pussy. He wanted her to orgasm once more.

Mia fell back to the bed. Out of the corner of his eye he saw her hand fist the blanket and smiled. She was trying to fight him so he didn't get what he wanted, but Curse wasn't taking no for an answer. Flicking her clit, he sucked the nub into his mouth and nibbled down on her body. Curse won the victory as she reached her second orgasm, coating his fingers in her cum.

Pulling back, he stared up into her dazed eyes, smiling.

"Well, baby, are you ready for a night of hard fucking?"

****

After everything she'd been through Mia didn't

think she'd be ready for having sex so soon after. But Dale hadn't sexually hurt her, and Curse never made her think of the other man. Where Dale was a cruel bastard, intent on hurting her, Curse was dominant, possessive, and he cared about her. Whenever she was around him, she felt loved and protected by him. He kissed her, and she tasted her cream on his lips.

Closing her eyes, she wrapped her arms around his neck. The bruises on her body didn't bother her, and they didn't have an effect on him. He saw past the purple marks that would all soon fade.

"Fuck me, Curse."

He dropped another kiss to her body, sliding between her legs as he did. She raked her nails down his back, needing to mark his body in some way so she knew who he belonged to.

Curse reared back. He gripped his cock, sliding the tip along her slit before going to her entrance. In one long thrust he seated himself to the hilt inside her.

"You're not wearing a condom."

"I'm not going to. You're probably pregnant anyway. There's no point us fighting what we both want."

She groaned as he gripped her hip and slid the last inch inside her, hitting the point where the pleasure and pain crashed together. Crying out, she pulled him back down, kissing his lips.

He spun them so she was on top of him.

"Let's see those tits bounce." Curse cupped her breasts, fingering her nipples. Bowing her head back, she arched her chest against his touch. "So fucking pretty. Ride my cock, baby. Show me how much you love dick."

Sliding up his length, she eased off then glided back down. Over and over she fucked his cock taking him all the way to the hilt inside her body. His hands went from her breasts to her hips, gripping them. When he couldn't stand her thrusts, he took over slamming all the way inside her. Curse didn't let up. He slammed up inside her as he brought her down on his cock.

She stared down into his eyes as he fucked her hard.

"No, I need more," he said.

He pulled her off his length and climbed out from under her. Mia was flipped to her knees, and he plunged inside her from behind.

"I like to watch my cock fucking your cunt. You open up around me and swallow me inside. Fuck, it looks so pretty. One day I'm going to fuck you while recording it so I can watch you again and again."

She shook her head. "No."

"Yes, and you won't deny me. I won't let you."

He spanked her ass twice. The heat went straight to her clit.

Moaning, she pushed back on his rock hard cock, wanting him to keep going inside her.

"You're so fucking tight. I'm going to have to keep taking you just to get you used to my length."

"Yes, please."

The sounds of their heavy breathing along with the slapping of naked bodies were the sounds echoing off the walls in the bedroom. Crying out, she was desperate to feel him explode inside her.

Curse rammed inside her.

"I'm so close to fucking coming. Come for me, Mia. Let me feel your cum."

Reaching between her thighs, she stroked her clit. Her body was so sensitive, and it didn't take more than a few strokes to take her over the edge into mindless pleasure.

She screamed as Curse grunted, fucking her

harder.

Within seconds his cock jerked within her, filling her cunt with his cum.

His fingers were almost bruising as they held her steady while he released inside her. "So perfect."

He collapsed over her, and her knees gave out. Falling to the bed, she felt his arms circle her body holding her tight.

"Give me a minute, baby. I'm catching my breath, and we'll do some more."

"You can go again?" she asked, teasing. His cock jerked inside her, and she wished she'd not said anything.

"I'm a member of the Chaos Bleeds, baby. I can go for a whole fucking lifetime."

She laughed. His arms banded around her body, and he kissed her neck.

"I don't doubt it."

"You shouldn't doubt anything I do. You're going to have to learn I tell the truth about most things." He sighed.

For several minutes they lay together, and she was at peace with his touch.

"Do you have a problem with what I did?" he asked.

Opening her eyes, she stared at the opposite wall. "No."

"Do you have any idea what I'm talking about?"

"I'm assuming this has to do with Dale. No, I don't have a problem with what you did to Dale. He deserved everything you did to him." She clenched her teeth together. "What about me?"

"Baby, I don't blame you for anything. You've put your life on hold because of what you did. I'll never tell anyone, and I'll make sure Ashley knows to keep shit to herself."

"You've got nothing to worry about. She won't tell anyone." Mia stroked his arm thinking about her friend. "I don't want you fucking her again."

"I won't. I didn't have you before." He kissed her neck. "We've got to find a place of our own."

"What about my mom? I can't just leave her."

"I'm not telling you to leave her, but we need a place to call our own." He pulled out of her body and stood from the bed. "Come on. We'll talk while we wash."

Taking his hand, she was conscious of his cum sliding down her thigh. Curse ran a bath and waited for her to get in before climbing in beside her. His arms rested along the edge of bathtub. She traced over each pattern and ink mark.

"Will I need to get a tattoo?" She'd never been a big fan of needles and didn't intend to start now.

"No. Some of the boys don't have ink. It's not a necessity."

She relaxed against his chest, feeling his cock pressing against her ass. "Don't you ever stop?" she asked, moaning.

"I like sex. I've been fucking for as long as I can remember."

Mia chuckled. "I'm going to walk funny if I don't find other ways to satisfy you."

He ran his hands down her body, fingering her breasts then going down to cup her pussy. "Don't you worry about a thing. I'll teach you to take my cock."

Turning in his arms, she reached down to grip his erection. Sliding her legs around his back, she eased up and then took his cock inside her.

Curse groaned. His hands went to her ass, gripping the flesh. "Baby, I think you're the one who's insatiable."

She grabbed a cloth and the soap. "I've got a reason. I want to wash you." Mia soaped the cloth and started to wipe his body.

He stroked her cheek, tracing over the marks.

Holding her breath, she waited for him to withdraw. He didn't scare her. Curse never frightened her.

"I wish he was still alive so I could hurt him some more."

She looked at his hands. The knuckles were cracked from the punches he'd given the man. Kissing the marks, Mia returned her gaze to his.

"No man has ever taken the time to protect me." She stared into his eyes. "We'll all be all right, right?"

He dropped his hand back to the side of the tub. "I don't know, baby. Jerry has his head stuck up his ass about this. I've not got a clue what's going to happen."

"I'm going to need to see my mom tomorrow."

"We're not going to let you die," Curse said.

"I know. I can't help but worry about it." She leaned forward and kissed his lips. Offering him a smile she washed his body as he started to thrust inside her.

"If you're going to have my cock inside you, you're going to fuck me as well."

Mia groaned as he jerked within her, hitting her cervix. The pleasure and pain combined.

"Yeah, that's what my baby wants. A nice hard fuck." His hands caressed over her front, pinching her nipples. The two pains combined together going straight to her clit at the sudden pulse of pleasure. "I can feel you squeezing me. You love my cock, don't you?"

"Yes, I love your cock."

"Then ride it."

"The water?" she said, moaning at the feel of him filling her.

"I don't give a fuck about the water. It can go anywhere. The only thing I give a fuck about is my cum inside your body."

His words were dirty and wrong, yet she couldn't stop the deep seated pleasure they created.

No longer caring about the mess, she gripped his shoulders and started to ride his cock. Curse sucked one of her nipples into his mouth. He bit down on the bud and licked the pain away.

"So beautiful. You better get used to being naked, baby."

Sinking her fingers into his hair, she tugged on the strands as she fucked his cock.

"Take your pleasure, Mia."

His cock went deep, and all she could do was fuck him.

They came together. Their release set the other off immediately.

Keeping her arms wrapped around him. Curse washed her body, and when they were finished he carried her through to the bedroom.

Staring into his eyes, Mia traced a finger over his lips.

"Don't leave me," she said.

"I won't."

"Everyone else has."

He shook his head. "Your father, weak shit that he is, left you. I never will." Curse claimed her lips, and she held him close. "No one is getting rid of me. You're my property, baby."

"I like that." She pressed her head against his and took several deep breaths. Yes, she could handle being Curse's property. For once, she wanted to let go, and the only person she trusted was Curse.

Chapter Eleven

Staring into his wardrobe, Curse placed the last dress he'd taken from Mia's house. Using the house to live in wasn't an option seeing as the club owned it and he was hogging it from the others. Devil didn't mind him spending time at the house, but his president made him aware of others needing it.

"How does Mia feel about moving in?" Ripper asked, leaning against the door to his room. He was at the clubhouse where a lot of the members were. Vincent kept stopping by along with Devil. Both men were clearly concerned about Frederick's visit to Piston County.

"She doesn't want to move in, but I'm not giving her a choice. This is where we're going to stay when we're not at her mother's." She wouldn't fuck when they were at her mother's. Mia had warned him that morning that she wouldn't ever be able to sleep with him with the risk of her mother hearing him.

"You're taking a lot of risk with this woman."

"What about Judi? Didn't you take a lot of risk with her?" He closed the wardrobe and turned to look at his friend. Curse had been the one Ripper called when Judi killed a man. He was able to clean a way a lot of mess. Dale wouldn't have been a problem if it wasn't for Jerry's involvement.

"She's different."

"No, she's not. She was the club princess. Devil's daughter and yet you fucked her."

"Shut the fuck up, Curse. You know not to say shit like that about my woman." Ripper was shaking his head. His hands were fisted at his sides.

"Then don't say shit about Mia. She's going to be my woman, and you'll show her the same kind of respect you're telling me to show Judi." Curse folded his arms over his chest.

"Judi was part of the club long before she became my old lady."

Curse shrugged. "I actually don't care. She won't say anything, and I love her."

The other man was silent as he let that bombshell out.

"You love her?"

"Yes, I'm in love with her, and when this visit is over we're getting married. That's how serious I am about all of this." Running fingers through his hair, he moved toward his free drawer and pulled out a fresh shirt. He was seeing Devil in a few minutes, and he wanted to be clean for when he went to Mia's place. They were spending the night with her mom.

"You're really serious about all this," Ripper said.

"I know. Who would have thought?"

"How's Ashley taking it?"

"She's taking it fine," Ashley said, rounding the corner. There was a smile on her lips. "Hey, can we talk?"

Curse looked at Ripper. "Are we done?"

"Yeah, we're done. I'll let Judi know you're getting married."

Before he could say anything Ripper was out of the door. Ashley chuckled.

"You're doomed now. Everyone will know and give you shit." She closed the door, giving them privacy.

"What's this all about?" he asked.

"I know Mia told you the truth, and I appreciate you not taking any anger out on her." Ashley locked her fingers in front of her. He noticed she wore long jeans and a shirt that didn't cling to her body. The sudden change in her clothes was a surprise.

"I wouldn't blame Mia for anything you've done.

What's going on?" He pointed at the clothes.

"I didn't feel like being on display. The club, Chaos Bleeds, you guys mean a lot to me. I know come Friday we're going to have some trouble heading our way. I don't want to stand out." She ran her palms down her thighs.

Curse knew she'd been talking with Devil and Jerry in private. He didn't know what about, but his suspicions rose.

"Honey, you're going to stand out."

Ashley was beautiful. He'd have to be blind not to see how beautiful she was, but his heart belonged to Mia.

"I'm going to do everything in my power to help you guys out on Friday."

"There's nothing you can do."

"I've been talking with Jerry and Devil. There might be something I can do. It's the least I can do."

Curse stared at her for several seconds. What could Jerry or Devil have said to her? Why would she do this?

"Why?" he asked.

"I owe Mia my life. Prom night was supposed to be the moment we moved on. She was going away to college, and I was going to join her to get away from my dad." Ashley shook her head. "He wasn't always a monster, but that's no excuse. She saved me that day and took a part of herself away. Mia sacrificed so much in her life." She licked her lips. "I'm sorry you don't get to see who she really was. There was a time when Mia would be so happy. She loved everything, life, family, dogs, pets, animals. Whoever was near her would be infected with such love. I took that away the day she killed my father."

"Why are you telling me this?" he asked, thinking

about Mia happy with life. There were a few times he saw the difference in her smile. He wondered what she was like when there wasn't a hardness in her eyes.

"Because I think the one person to help her is you. If anyone can bring Mia back to life properly, it's you."She stepped closer to him. Ashley took hold of his hand and smiled. "I'm happy knowing you'll take care of her."

She kissed his cheek and withdrew from him.

"Take care of her."

"I will."

Ashley left his room without another word. Touching his cheek, he wondered what the hell was going on with her. She left his room without a backward glance.

He pushed his concern to the back of his mind and went down to the office where Devil was waiting for him. Pussy was in the office along with Death, Vincent, and Ripper.

"What's going on?" he asked.

"We're having a meeting concerning this meeting Friday. Jerry is concerned. In fact, we're all concerned. I put a call through to Alex, Tiny's former brother-in-law," Devil said.

Curse closed the door and took a seat next to Pussy. "What did he say? I take it it's not good news."

"Frederick Gonzalez is not a man to be taken lightly. Most people, the law, criminals, bikers, you name it, most of them keep a wide berth of this man." Devil stood away from the desk. "He's known everywhere for having his fingers in so many pies. Alex hasn't done deals with him, but he knows of him. The Skulls stay away from him."

"What pies does he have?" Curse asked.

"Everything," Jerry said.

Jerking around he saw the drug dealing pimp stood in the doorway. He closed the door and walked further into the room. "I figured you'd need me here to help you with this. Planning for his visit won't do you any good."

"We're not planning anything. We're talking." Devil stared at the other man.

"How did you come to deal with Frederick?" Curse asked, curious to know how someone so powerful would be in Piston County. Vegas made sense along with all the cities, not this small town.

"Frederick knows to have contacts in many places. I used to be part of his bigger circle. We moved around a lot, across America, Europe, you name it, he got stronger. It originally started with his dad being a small town crime man. Over the years his father built it up until Frederick killed his father to take over. He has branched over the world. No one can touch him, and anyone who tries to take him on ends up dead. It's either join him or die trying to get away from him." Jerry walked toward the whisky decanter and poured himself a generous shot.

"You're nervous about this?" Devil asked.

"I've not seen him in a long time. This is my area, and one of the men he wanted to kill was taken from him. Frederick is many things, but forgiving is not one of them." Jerry swigged down the large shot of whisky. "We've got two choices. One, he will come to hate us on sight and kill all of us including our families, or he'll bring you into the family, which means you're going to help him when he needs it without any questions asked."

"We're not some fucking taxi service, Jerry. I don't answer to anyone."

"He doesn't care. Frederick will get what he wants, and we either follow his lead or we die." Jerry poured himself another drink.

"None of them are an option. We're not going to die, and we're not going to be used as puppets." Devil slammed his palm on the table. "Do not ever say shit like that. Nothing will happen to Lexie and my kids. Do you understand me?"

Jerry shrugged. "Do I look like I care right now? We're all fucked. A word of warning to you all, I've sent my woman away. Anyone you want out of harm's away do it now." Jerry slammed the glass down on the desk, leaving them.

"He's charming," Pussy said. "Why don't we kill him as well?"

"Shut it, Pussy. Alex warned me about this. Frederick is a fair man, but he doesn't take shit lightly. He's going to want something from us." Devil sat down, locking his hands together.

"So, what do we do?" Ripper asked. "I don't think I'm the only one who's concerned. I've got Judi to think about."

"This is all my fault. Offer him the chance to kill me," Curse said.

"No, I'm not doing that. Dale Worthington was a sick fuck who deserved to die. No, we're going to have to stay together as a unit. We'll apologize, but we're not handing any of our men over. I'm not into that kind of shit. I've been talking with Gonzalez through Jerry. We've got something in the works, and hopefully it will take care of some of our problems." Devil slammed his palm on the desk. "Get out and do what you need to do. I'm going to take care of Lexie and let her know what's happening." Devil looked at Ripper. "Tell Judi the same."

Leaving the room, Curse went to his bike. He was going to spend some time with Mia and her mother before Friday.

****

"Baby, what happened?" Mia's mother, Debra, asked. Curse had taken some of her clothes out. When Mia had entered her home she'd shouted for her mother not to get up. After sending him away with some of her own clothes she'd made two cups of tea and entered her mother's room.

Debra lay amongst plenty of pillows. There was some color in her cheeks, which filled Mia with hope.

"Nothing. Forget about the bruises. How have you been?" Mia asked.

"No, you don't get to do that to me, missy. You will tell me everything that happened or I will grab the phone and call everyone I know."

"One of the clients I worked for thought he could touch me. Curse arrived, and he saved me from what the guy did. He's handling it."

Her mother looked at her doubtfully.

"Please, Mom, let it go. Curse saved me from something terrible. Trust me."

"Fine. I hate this. I want you to know that, and when I see Curse he better let me know what he intends to do. I may be sick, but I'll take care of my baby any way I can."

Chuckling, she tried to direct her mother to talking about Curse, but her mother wasn't easily fooled.. She hoped her mother didn't ask more questions after this.

"Well, this client person better know to leave this town before I get my hands on him. I won't be in bed forever, Mia. How dare he touch my little girl?" Debra grabbed Mia's face and kissed her head. "I've missed you. Now that I've had my say you can tell me about this man. Bradley James, he's such a nice man."

"Curse?"

"Yes, I don't like calling him Curse. It's wrong. There is nothing to curse a man like him. He's too much of a nice young man to be thought of as a curse. Honey, you've got yourself a keeper."

Chuckling, she curled up against her mother. "I love him, Mom. He makes me feel sexy and loved."

"Any man who leaves you feeling like that is a keeper. You need to snatch him up before another woman tries to do the same." Debra stroked her hair.

"I'm not going to let him get away," Mia said.

She nibbled her lip as doubt started to set in.

"What's going on in that mind of yours?" Debra asked.

"I was thinking about Dad. I mean, I thought he loved us enough and that he'd never leave, but that's not true."

"Don't do that, Mia." Debra stroked her cheek, forcing her to look up. "Your father and I loved each other when it was necessary. Don't try and make our relationship something it wasn't. I love you, honey, but you're wrong about a lot of things."

"What do you mean?"

"I stopped loving your father a long time ago. He was a great dad but not a great husband. We'd been living separate lives for a long time. You just didn't notice it." Debra smiled at her. "You and Bradley are the real deal. I see that look in your eyes, and I know I never felt that deeply for any man. You're lucky, Mia. Don't let fear of what happened between your father and me cloud your own feelings."

Sometime later, Mia was putting some finishing touches to the pasta she'd made as Curse walked into the house. There was no mistaking the masculine sigh that greeted her. Smiling, she tossed the salad together and put some on a plate for her mother.

He rounded the corner, removing his jacket.

"Hey, babe, sorry I'm late."

"No need to be sorry. The talk ran a little longer than you expected?" she asked, putting his food on the table.

"Yeah." He took a seat as she picked up the tray.

"I'm just going to take this up to Mom. Are you going to start without me, Bradley?" she asked, chuckling as he glared at her.

"Only nice people get to call me that."

"I'm a nice person."

"No, you're a naughty person. I believe you've had your ass spanked a couple of times in the last week."

She didn't expect his words, and heat filled her cheeks. Entering her mother's room, she placed the tray on her lap.

"Was that Bradley I heard?"

"Yeah, he'll be up to see you shortly."

"I'm going to get better, Mia. Everything is going to be good, I promise you."

Kissing her mother's cheek Mia agreed. For the first time since her father left, Mia really did believe everything was going to be all right.

Going back downstairs she found Curse getting himself a second portion. "I was feeding you and you could cook like this?"

"You never asked for me to cook. I did what I was told, and you told me to sit on my ass and let you cook." Picking up her fork, she started to eat as Curse joined her. He lifted her leg up to rest on his lap. With his free hand, he caressed up her calf.

"I'm not going to sleep with you," she said.

"We're not sleeping. You didn't say anything about having fun." He dropped his fork and turned the paper she hadn't noticed on the table for her to look at.

SAM CRESCENT

"What do you think of an apartment?"

She looked down at a picture of one of the luxury places near the wealthy part of Piston County.

"Erm, I can't afford it, Curse." One of the men she cleaned for was dead. Her mother's medical bills were a constant concern.

"Baby, I've got plenty saved up. We can afford this, and we won't have to worry about rent. I'll buy it outright. I've never had a problem with drugs or drink. I've got plenty of money." He gave her a smile.

His touch caressed up the inside of her thigh. Curse didn't go further up, and he kept teasing her with whatever else he could do.

After they were finished with food, Curse went to grab her mother's tray, and she washed the dishes. He surprised her by grabbing a towel and drying up the dishes.

"When we get our own place you can cook every day."

"I can't cook every day. Curse, this is insane. How can I move in with you? You'll be paying for everything." She ran fingers through her hair as she stared at him.

"We'll be a couple, and soon we'll be married. What I have is yours." He placed the towel in the washing machine, taking hold of her arm and drawing her closer to him. The scent of leather filled her nostrils, turning her on.

He cupped her cheek, stroking a thumb along her lips. She opened her mouth, and he slid his thumb inside. With his other hand, he tugged at the button holding her jeans up.

"Curse, what are you doing?" she asked.

"I'm going to fuck you. Your mother was already asleep when I left the room. No one can hear us."

She couldn't deny him. Her body was on fire for his touch.

Wriggling out of the jeans, she tore at his clothes as he got her naked. He lifted her up and placed her on the kitchen counter. His lips were on her pussy before she could stop him. Gripping his hair, she smashed her pussy against his face needing the slight edge of pain to the pleasure.

"That's it, baby, take what you want." He slammed fingers inside her as he sucked in her clit.

As she cried out, the pleasure was too much.

"No, I want to feel your cunt around my cock before you come."

He stood, pulled his cock out of the slit in the jeans. She watched him rub the tip up and down her slit before thrusting deep into her core. Sinking her nails into his bare shoulders, she pressed her lips to his neck to keep her noises down. Mia sucked on his neck wanting to mark his flesh for others to know who he belonged to.

"You're so fucking tight. I can't wait to get inside your ass. You're going to love my cock there."

Curse bit her nipples, sliding his tongue over the peaks to ease out the sting. He pulled her off the counter and slammed in deep. They both cried out together. Holding onto the counter, she thrust down onto his cock. The angle was odd, but he got so deep inside her.

"We're going to need to do something about this," she said. "You never wear a condom."

"I never want to wear one. I don't care if I get you pregnant. That's how much I want you, Mia. I want you pregnant with my kid. You'll make a good mother. I want everything from you. Your laughter, your screams of pleasure and pain. Give me everything."

He was asking for her to give a part of herself she'd not even thought about in such a long time. Ever since her life had been changed by taking a life she'd kept the happiness from inside her.

"Please, give it to me, Mia." He cupped her face, pressing his lips to hers.

Could she do it?

Why are you hiding?

Nodding her head, she smiled. "Yes, Curse, I'll give you everything."

He fucked her harder, going deep inside her. She forgot where she was and gave him everything he wanted. Opening up her feelings, she fucked Curse, loving him with every part of her being.

When he pulsed deep inside her as she came to a screaming orgasm, she wrapped her arms around him. Curse held her as he carried her through to the sitting room.

His hands caressed up and down her back, comforting her in ways she didn't think was possible.

"You're never going to regret giving me what I need."

"Please, don't hurt me," she said.

Curse pushed some of her hair off her shoulder. "Baby, the one thing you can fucking guarantee, I will never hurt you. I will protect and love you for the rest of my natural born fucking life."

He tugged her head down and claimed her lips. Moaning, Mia finally felt alive. For so long she'd been dying inside from what happened. Curse loved her and made her feel safe to finally be herself. He kissed across her neck to her ear.

"No one will ever find him, Mia. The club and I will always make sure you're protected." As he nibbled her ear, she giggled.

"When you two have stopped screwing, could I have my water and pills?" Debra asked, shouting downstairs for them to hear.

Gasping, Mia turned to look at Curse.

"I thought she was asleep. She must have been fibbing."

"You did that on purpose," Mia said, slapping his arm.

"I'm a guy. Never trust a horny guy, Mia. He'll say anything to get you in bed." Shaking her head, she wrapped her arms around his neck.

"I'll remember that for the future." Her heart was racing, but she couldn't stop smiling.

Chapter Twelve

Friday

The tension in the club could be felt. Lexie was standing by Devil's side as Phoebe was with Vincent. Judi and Ripper were missing, and Curse found out that the other man was on babysitting duty. Devil still considered Judi a baby and wouldn't have her anywhere near the club when problems could occur.

Mia stood beside him. She kept playing with her shirt, tugging on the end and moving from side to side. Her fidgeting didn't bother him. Curse couldn't blame her. This Frederick Gonzalez had been given some kind of monster reputation.

Many of the men were playing cards or shooting pool.

"This is horseshit," Pussy said. "I'm not going to be stressing out about this. Devil, what do you think of the idea of having some prospects around?"

"You're really going to talk about this now?" Jerry asked.

"Look, before we settled down here we were on the road. I'm not used to being scared. I refuse to be scared of a man who can die from a fucking bullet just like everyone else. We've got business of our own. I say we handle that shit before we all drive each other crazy over what could happen."

Out of all of the men, Pussy didn't have a filter from his brain to his mouth. Curse recalled all the men they'd ended up fighting because Pussy couldn't stop talking.

"He's got a point," Death said. "We can sit here worrying, or we can do what we do best and consider this a party."

"Prospects?" Lexie asked. "Do I even want to know?"

"You were a stripper, Lex. You could give us some entertainment."

Devil grabbed the nearest beer bottle and threw it at Death for his comment.

"Hey, I was being nice. Your woman knew how to dance," Death said, laughing.

"Stop it, Death, while you still have your cock attached," Lexie said, snuggling against Devil. With his arms busy holding his woman, he couldn't start throwing things or hurting others.

Wrapping his own arms around Mia, Curse watched his club. They were a family in their way. They were not perfect, nor were they monsters. Chaos Bleeds lived by their own code, a code of the road and of a brotherhood, similar to The Skulls only not as harsh on the rules.

"Devil," Snake said. "Three cars have just pulled into the lot. They're locking the front gates."

Glancing down at Mia, Curse smiled at his woman.

"Four men are guarding the gates, and several men are coming to the door. I think this is show time," Snake said.

Jerry moved to the window. "Yep, that's Frederick."

"The guy in the suit with the fancy haircut?" Snake said. "He looks more like a businessman than anything else."

"Yeah, that's him."

The doors to the club opened. Two large men entered. Their hands were down their sides, but the tension was easy to see.

Another couple of men entered the club and

started to look around the building.

"What do you think you're doing?" Devil asked.

"They're checking your place for anyone hoping to kill me," Frederick said. He had an Italian accent but spoke perfect English and was easily understood.

"Pussy, Death, go and follow them." Devil sent the two men off to follow the other men.

Watching everything play out, Curse gripped Mia's shoulder to stop her from moving or catching any of the men's eyes.

"So, this is the clubhouse of Devil, Chaos Bleeds MC leader. It's nice, if a little, should I say, clichéd." Frederick walked over to the bar, whistling. "At least you're fully stocked on the good stuff. Pour me a whisky, straight. I want the aged stuff, none of the shit people like to serve in crap bars."

"You're insulting my hospitality," Devil said. "Call your dogs off or else."

"Your hospitality?" Frederick chuckled. He poured himself a drink and turned to look at Jerry. "You think this is your town? You're wrong. Now, Fort Wills is owned by Tiny and The Skulls. They own that town outright, and even I won't mess with that kind of shit. No drugs and no women and I respect that. This town, however, this town is mine." He turned to look at the room.

Curse saw the smile on his lips, the cruelty. The insult was clear for all of them to see. Frederick respected Tiny while he didn't respect Devil or the club.

Devil looked ready to commit murder.

"Now, I let Rob slide—and yes, I knew about you then—because he was a little shit upstart who thought he was better than anyone else. Dale I was looking forward to hurting, and you took that opportunity away from me. Not only was I going to give him to a friend but I was getting a shitload of money from him. I want to know why, and you better have a damn good reason." He took a sip of the whisky. "Damn, that's good."

"I'm the reason Dale was killed," Mia said, stepping forward.

Curse swore as she brought the guy's attention toward her. The bruises had lessened slightly but not much.

"Come here," Frederick said.

Going with her, Curse refused to be pushed aside.

"You're the one who killed him?"

"Yes."

"Figured as much." Frederick grabbed her face, turned it this way and that. "Dale was an animal. He couldn't handle being told no. What else did he do to you?"

"He tried to rape me. Curse got there before he could do that," she said, looking down at the floor.

"Fine. I can see why you killed the fucker. I know Dale had already raped a couple of women, and then he nearly fucked up the deal that you guys did by raping my friend's daughter. Any man who needs to rape a woman is no man in my book. Now, beating a woman from time to time is okay. They need to be kept in line. Raping, I don't like or agree with." He dropped his hand. "Go away."

Curse despised the man. No man should ever lay a hand on a woman to cause her pain.

The men who'd gone away to look around the clubhouse came back holding Ashley's arm. She wasn't fighting them. Pussy and Death looked annoyed as they followed behind them. None of them were used to having to follow other men around.

Holding onto Mia, Curse watched the conversation.

"Now, I'm a lenient man, but I can be pushed. I accept why Dale had to die, but we've got to come to some arrangement," Frederick said, facing Devil. "Jerry told me you're businessmen and you won't make waves unless you have to."

"We are businessmen. We're not lapdogs," Devil said.

"Good, I'm not looking for lapdogs. I'm looking for men who can do a job without getting caught." Frederick took a seat, looking more relaxed than tense. "I think we can do business providing you're prepared to listen to me."

"What do you want us to do?" Devil asked.

"I like Tiny. He's a good man and has morals. I want you to make sure Piston County remains your town. Any new little upstart you take out, and we take their business. I want you to run guns and drugs. The women I'm not interested in yet. I've got plenty of girls around the world earning me more than enough money. However, that may change as all business does." Frederick took another sip. "I want you to do a better job than the person I've got in charge now."

"Frederick, I—" Jerry started to speak.

Curse tensed and covered Mia's mouth as Frederick shot Jerry without another word. The bullet entered the front of his head and smashed the window behind him. Jerry fell to the floor. Lexie screamed, covering her ears, and Phoebe cried out. The whole room stayed silent.

Turning toward his president he saw Devil gritting his teeth at the slight they'd been dealt with. Jerry had never been a problem to any of them, and now he was dead.

"As you can see I've got a job opening for a new leader of Piston County," Frederick said.

Ashley looked pale, ready to pass out.

"You're fucking insane," Devil said.

"I can kill you all now, and when I'm done here I can go and get Judi and Ripper, I believe his name is. I can kill all of your family, and I couldn't give a shit."

"How can I trust you not to do that to us?" Devil asked.

"You're friends with Tiny. I suggest you start taking a leaf out of his book and own this fucking town once and for all." Frederick looked at all of the men in turn. "Now, are you willing to agree to my terms, or is this a waste of my time? I've got the girl. You, Jerry, and myself have already agreed to her."

"We need time to vote," Devil said.

They were all trapped. There was no choice.

"I vote yes," Curse said. Everyone turned to look at him. He hoped the others knew what he was doing.

Pussy and Death agreed. Others started to nod their agreement.

"It looks like we're the new Sheriffs in town," Devil said.

"Good, I'll take her with me now as well." Frederick pointed at Ashley. "I like to look at her from the picture you sent me. We've got a deal."

Curse looked at Ashley. She seemed to know this was going to happen.

"We only talked about you agreeing to take her. It wasn't confirmed. I can't allow you to take a woman without her consent." Devil took a step away from Lexie.

"I'm going to go," Ashley said. Her voice was small, but her tone said to all of them not to argue. "It's time for me to move on, and I already talked with Jerry and Frederick about mending fences for the Chaos Bleeds crew."

"Ashley, no," Mia said.

"I've got to, honey. Jerry told me this could happen. He even suggested it to me. It's time for me to get out of here, and I was already going to go." She moved toward Mia. Curse let his woman go for a few minutes to allow the two women to hug. "I'm dying here. This is not my home."

"I don't want you to go."

"We'll stay in touch. I promise you, I'll be more than fine." Ashley kissed her cheek. "Take care of her."

"I will," Curse said.

He watched as Ashley said goodbye to the club. She was giving up her freedom to help the club. This was why she'd come to him the other day to ask him to take care of Mia. Curse wanted to tell her to stop, but he couldn't.

"I want to do this," Ashley said. She moved toward Frederick's side. All of the club watched the other man nod to his men.

****

"You can't do this," Mia said. Ashley simply smiled at her.

"Yes, I can. I can do what I want. You're taken care of, and I've got nothing to worry about. Curse loves you, and I'll be back in time for the wedding." Ashley kissed her forehead. "You need to move on, and so do I."

Mia's heart was breaking. "I don't want you to go."

"I know, but I want to go just like you wanted to go to college, Mia." Ashley wrapped her arms around her. Curse stepped back, giving them space.

"I love you," Mia said.

"I love you. You're my best friend, and I promise I'll be fine. More than fine. You've got nothing to be afraid of."

"She will be allowed to communicate with you,"

Frederick said, clearing his throat. Mia looked over her friend's shoulder at the handsome man waiting to take her away.

"You'll take good care of her?" Mia asked.

"I will. Regardless of what people think I don't make a habit of killing women myself." Frederick gripped Ashley's arm. Mia noticed he didn't say anything about employing men to kill women for him.

"Jerry organized it with me," Ashley said, turning to look at Devil. "I know you didn't want us to do this after we talked, but we did."

The president of the Chaos Bleeds nodded at Ashley. Mia watched it all feeling helpless.

"I look forward to doing business with you. I advise that you get rid of that body and pick up where Jerry left off," Frederick said, flicking his wrist at the dead body of Jerry, the pimp.

Mia couldn't look at him. Jerry didn't deserve to die, but she was glad it was none of the people Curse cared about.

He gripped her shoulders, tugging her back against him. "Don't worry about her."

"I won't." Mia would always worry about her friend.

Within twenty minutes Frederick was gone, yet the tension in the clubhouse remained. Vincent was trying to calm Phoebe down. Lexie was crying and snuggled in close to Devil. Not one brother made a sound. Her throat felt tight, and her vision blurred as the tears started to build.

"She did us all a favor," Pussy said.

"Jerry knew something bad was going to happen," Devil said. "He probably didn't expect to be killed. I knew Ashley was going to go. She came to me with Jerry's plan."

Turning toward the older man, Mia stared at him waiting.

"What do you mean?" Curse asked.

"Ashley spent time with Jerry and found out more about Frederick. It seems the pimp talked a lot with drink in his system. She offered to go with Frederick in the hope of helping us. She even talked with him."

"How is she going to help?" Mia asked. "She's just Ashley. She's stupid and impulsive." She shook her head. "You shouldn't have let her go."

Curse pulled her close, turning her against his chest. She gripped his jacket sobbing.

"Your friend is a lot of things, Mia. Stupid isn't one of them. We've now got a woman on the inside. Ashley showed us loyalty, and she will not betray us," Devil said.

"What do you mean?" This came from Pussy.

"It means until further notice we're Frederick Gonzalez's lapdogs. We do what he says when he says it, and we keep our fucking heads down." Devil held his woman close to him. "The visit with The Skulls is important. I want you all present in the house when the barbeque happens. They're going to help us."

"What was that shit with Tiny?" Death asked.

"He's trying to separate us. Control us and in the end, rule over us," Devil said. "This is not your backdoor drug dealer or your pimp. He knows his power and intends to use it. We've all got to be ready for what's going to come our way. It could be a month, a couple of months, years, I don't know. What I do know is that we all have to band together. No secrets, no shit."

The room agreed with Devil on the future plans. Mia stared at Jerry's body, feeling the weight of the words spoken on her shoulders.

"We need to clean this mess up," Curse said.

Everyone started moving at once. Curse took her hand and led her upstairs.

"Where are we going?" she asked.

"You've cleaned away enough blood and dead bodies to last you a lifetime. I'm not going to let you do anymore." He opened the door to a bedroom. "This is my room."

"I need to help."

"No, you need to rest. I'm not taking no for an answer. You can fight with me all you want. This is not going to change shit."

Running fingers through her hair she stepped into his room. The scent was entirely of him. "This is where you live?"

"For now at least. I'm still looking at that apartment. In fact, I got a viewing next week."

"Curse, are you ready for this?" she asked, sitting down on his bed.

"I think the question is, are you ready for this?"

"What do you mean?"

He knelt down in front of her. Curse ran his hands up and down her thighs. "For a long time you've pushed men away. Don't get me wrong, I love the fact no one knows how awesome you are in bed." She hit out at him, smiling. "But you're mine, Mia, and I'm laying my claim. Once we move in together, we'll be getting married and you'll be having my kids. I don't care about anything else, just you." He touched her cheek, running his fingers down to her lip. "Are you ready to be claimed?"

She nodded without hesitation. The only man she ever felt comfortable with was Curse. "Yes, I want to be caught and claimed."

"Then consider yourself taken." He pressed his lips to hers.

Opening her mouth, she met his tongue with her own.

"I love you," she said when he withdrew.

"I better go and help the club before they get pissed at me. Have a shower and relax. The television is over there. I'll be back." Curse kissed her head and left the room.

Sitting on the bed for several minutes she looked around his space. The room was very personal to him yet bare at the same time. He was clean at least.

She stood up and went into the bathroom. Stripping down, she took a long shower, closing her eyes to face up to the spray of the jet. The warmth seeped into her bones, relaxing her.

"I thought I'd find you here," Curse said.

Gasping, she turned to see him already naked.

"I thought you were going to take longer," she said.

"It has been an hour, babe. What have you been doing?" He took the cloth from her and started to wash her body. She'd already washed but didn't care. His touch awakened the fire inside her.

"Nothing, I've been thinking about us and our future."

"Good. We'll hold off on the wedding until we know more from Ashley." Curse dropped the cloth onto the tiled floor and placed his hand between her thighs. "I want you to come on my fingers."

Turning toward him, she reached for his rock hard cock. "Then I expect the same from you." She worked his thick length, moaning as two fingers slid inside her pussy and his thumb pressed to her clit.

"Go on, baby. Take what you want. You want my cum, then work for it."

She opened her legs giving him better access to

her core. Cupping his balls, she stared into his eyes loving how they dilated as they looked at her.

"This is it now, baby. No one else is going to know how hot you are," he said.

"I'm glad. The same goes for you. No other woman is going to know how hard your cock gets."

Crying out, she released his balls to grip his shoulder to keep herself from falling. His other hand gripped her hip, pushing her against the wall.

"Come for me, Mia."

He stroked her pussy in time with her strokes around his cock.

Moaning, she felt the first stirring of her arousal.

"I'm here, Mia. I'm going to catch you."

Screaming, she came over his hand. Curse grunted, and she stared down to see his cum explode over her stomach. Biting her lip, she felt him shake.

Together, they stopped moving, and she stared into his eyes.

"Thank you," she said, resting her head against his chest.

"Baby, there's no need to thank me." He kissed the top of her head. She stayed still as he washed the semen from her stomach.

Once they were done, Curse took over, drying her body before helping her into a towel. Together they went to his bed without wearing any clothes.

"What's going on in that head of yours?" he asked.

"Nothing. I hope Ashley is okay and that I'm not going to have to be standing by her graveside."

"Ashley's many things, but she's not stupid. Whatever she's doing is safe." He kissed her head, wrapping his arms around her. "Get some sleep. I'll be here for you in the morning."

Chapter Thirteen

Three weeks later

Curse stood back from the sitting room in the apartment he and Mia now owned. They'd settled, and he paid for the place the moment he saw how much Mia liked it. All they needed to do was make the space theirs. Decorating was something he hated, but to see her smile, he'd do it.

"Hey, baby, I brought pizza," Mia said.

"Pizza?" Pussy, Devil, and Death all asked.

He walked out of the sitting room he was painting in a cream color to find Mia, Judi, and Lexie carrying boxes of pizza. The smell was heavenly. He placed the paintbrush on the floor where a piece of paper was laid.

Walking to his woman, he wrapped his arms around her and claimed her lips. "You know I love you right?"

"You're not getting out of decorating. I stopped by Mom's place, and she's organizing the wedding. I think it has given her a new whole lease of life." Mia stroked a finger down his newest piece of ink. On his chest, he'd gotten her name printed over his heart.

"I love it. I, erm, I booked an appointment to get your name inked just here." She took his hand and placed it along the base of her back. "Lexie told me you guys love that."

His cock hardened. "You're going to have my name on your ass."

"Every time you take me from behind you'll see your name staring back at you."

"Get the fuck out," Curse said. "Take the pizza and fucking leave."

"Curse—"

The men were smirking as they headed out of the apartment. Devil, Pussy, and Death were laughing on their way out of the front door.

"I can't believe you just did that."

He didn't give her a chance to say anything. He stripped the clothes from her body before the door even closed. The only pizza in the house was from the box she'd picked up.

"Shut up. You're the one who started talking about ink and getting my name put on your body. This is your punishment for teasing me. I'm going to fuck that very ass I've been preparing for myself."

Mia groaned, tearing at his body. He moved her toward the front room where he'd stored the tube of lube in the shopping bag he'd bought that morning before she woke up.

"Where are we going? Don't we need to get to the bedroom?"

"Not got time for the bedroom." There was no bed in their room, and the mattress was on the floor. Bending her over the sofa, he stared at the rounded curve or her ass where he saw his name written on with marker.

"Who did this?" he asked.

"Lexie did. She told me you'd love to see it." His president's woman was a dangerous person. With his cock rock hard, he aligned the tip to her pussy and slid in deep.

He grabbed the tube of lubrication as she screamed from his penetration. Pulling back, he slammed back inside her.

Squirting plenty of lubrication on his fingers, he teased the lube against her ass, sliding a finger in deep.

She took his finger without pain. He'd been working dildos of many sizes up inside her so she wouldn't be afraid to take his cock.

After she took three of his fingers, he slid out of her cunt to smear the remaining lube over his length. Once he was covered with plenty of gel he started to work his cock in deep inside her ass. At first she tightened around his length but he reached around and started to rub her clit. She came apart in a matter of seconds and while she screamed in pleasure, and he thrust all of his cock into her ass.

Staring at his name, Curse knew when she got the ink on her back, he wasn't going to want to fuck her any other way. Tracing over the lines, he waited for her to get accustomed to his dick.

"Your ass is so fucking hot. I'm not going to want to fuck any other part of you." Spanking her ass, he watched the pale skin turn a nice shade of red.

"Please, Curse, fuck me. I'm desperate."

Chuckling, he spread the cheeks of her ass wide to watch his cock slide in and out of her warmth.

"Are you watching?" she asked.

"Yes, you should see how fucking hot you look taking my cock." He fucked her slowly, prolonging the pleasure and making it painful for him. His balls felt blue from having to wait so long to claim her.

"How does it feel?" he asked.

"So good," she said, groaning.

Biting her lip, she thrust back against him. Curse gripped her hips and worked his cock out of her ass only to plunge back inside. Together they both groaned and screamed at the pleasure.

"Touch your clit, baby, I want to feel you come."

She started to tease her clit, and he worked her anus with his cock. Closing his eyes, he gave her everything he had. Within minutes she splintered apart and her ass tightened around him setting off his own orgasm.

Curse growled as he released inside her ass. She collapsed over the sofa as he wrapped his arms around her.

"I can't move," she said, seconds later.

"Don't worry. We're going to have to move for the guys to come back." He kissed the back of her neck, sucking on the delicate flesh of her neck.

"Come back?" she asked, tensing.

"Yeah, do you really think I'm going to do all of this decorating myself?" He eased out of her and picked her up in his arms. "Besides, you look adorable in jeans and a shirt with spattered paint." He carried her into the bathroom and turned the shower on.

"How can you kick them out and then invite them back inside? Don't you think that's rude?"

"Babe, Devil kicks us out of his place when he wants to fuck his woman. In fact, he makes us watch the kids when he wants to screw her."

"So? It doesn't mean that we have to be the same," she said.

"When you blush, it's the cutest thing I've ever seen." He kissed her nose and then proceeded to wash her body. Curse wrapped his arms around her body, laughing at her embarrassment.

"It's so cute that you're embarrassed, but I can tell you, it's wrong. The men know you're going to have been fucked good. Now, I suggest you smile and pretend they're only just arriving." He turned the shower off.

She caught him unawares as she wrapped her arms around him.

"I love you, Curse."

"Babe, I can't even find the right fucking words to describe how I feel about you." He caught her ass toward him. "You're getting the ink, and I'm going to be there to make sure the fucker doesn't get it wrong."

Claiming her lips, Curse knew his life was complete with Mia in it.

Epilogue

One month later

"Do you miss me, baby?" Pussy asked, walking down the main street in Piston County's town center.

"I miss the club. The sun and heat are a nice change. You're going into fall, right?" Ashley asked.

He'd kept in touch with Ashley since she left with Frederick. Pussy didn't like the thought of anything happening to her. She wasn't the woman he was going to fall in love with, but Pussy cared about her, and they were good friends. He knew what Mia had done for her. Ashley had told him one night when no one was around and he'd talked about his less than stellar upbringing.

"I bet the women are glad to see me gone," Ashley said.

"Hardly, you're the only woman who could satisfy me. You're coming down for the wedding in a couple of months, right?"

"Yeah, Frederick is already making arrangements. He wants to come and see as well." She sighed over the line. "Is Mia happy?"

"She's happy to be in love, and when I see her with Curse, she's always smiling. I take back the cold ice princess remarks. She's all warm and fuzzy." Pussy paused as he spotted Sasha Carmichael leaning against a wall. Her hands were fisted at her sides, and she looked to be having a panic attack. "The Skulls are coming for the wedding as well. Lash and Angel should be around for it, too."

"Good, I've got to go, Pussy. Please keep in touch. I miss you."

"Miss you, too, babe."

He closed his cell phone, watching the young girl.

Glancing past her and around the street he expected to see her stepfather or her mother. No one was in sight.

Frowning, he approached the girl. For some reason, he didn't like seeing her upset.

"Who's there?" she asked, the moment he got close.

"It's okay, babe, are you okay?"

She stared at his chest and frowned.

"Who are you? I don't recognize your voice."

Her brown hair caught the sun and the length looked full and glossy. The urge to reach out and stroke the strands suddenly struck him hard.

"The name's Pu—Shane Wilkins. I'm part of the Chaos Bleeds crew."

"The biker group that has everyone in a fit?" she asked, still looking at his chest.

"Honey, you got a problem with looking me in the face?" he asked, getting annoyed. Was she too good to look him in the eyes?

Her cheeks went pink. "I'm so sorry. I thought I was."

"Unbelievable."

Pussy went to walk away annoyed with the rebuke when she reached out. Her hand encountered thin air, and she reached out again. The frustration was easy for him to see.

"Please, I'm not being mean, I promise. Erm, I'm blind. I can't see anything." She looked left then right, and it was then Pussy recognized her reactions. The noises were quiet, but she kept her eyes focused in front of her. They were pretty eyes, but they didn't see a thing.

"Sasha, honey." A male voice interrupted the moment. He recognized the stepfather Ashley hated. Sasha tensed, and her nails sank into his flesh. The fear was evident in her tense posture as her stepfather approached. "Get your grubby hands off my daughter."

Stepping back, Pussy stared at the young girl, the young blind girl who was terrified of the man coming to take her. The protective instincts inside him rose, and all he wanted to do was stop the man from taking her.

There was nothing for him to do but watch her leave. Within seconds, Sasha Carmichael had impacted his world, and he didn't know what he was going to do.

Yeah, he did. Pussy was going to do everything in his power to protect her.

The End

www.samcrescent.com

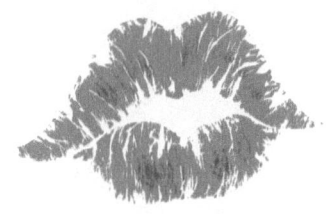

EVERNIGHT PUBLISHING ®

www.evernightpublishing.com

www.ingramcontent.com/pod-product-compliance
Lightning Source LLC
Chambersburg PA
CBHW022130170626
46808CB00002B/925